THE DSA SEASON TWO, BOOK ONE

# THE WELLSPRING

## Lou Paduano

Eleven Ten Publishing LLC

GRAND ISLAND, NEW YORK

Copyright © 2023 by Lou Paduano
All rights reserved. This book or any portion thereof may not be reproduced or used in any manner whatsoever without the express written permission of the publisher except for the use of brief quotations in a book review.

Eleven Ten Publishing LLC
282 Fareway Lane
Grand Island, NY 14072

Publisher's note: This is a work of fiction. Names, characters, places, and incidents either are the product of the author's imagination or are used fictitiously. Any resemblance to actual events, locales, or persons, living or dead, is entirely coincidental.

Printed in the United States of America
Edited by JP Services.
Cover art design by MiblArt

First edition published 2023

Library of Congress Cataloging in Publication Data
Paduano, Lou
The Wellspring / Lou Paduano

LCCN: 2023914022
ISBN-13: 978-1-944965-31-0 (paperback)
ISBN-13: 978-1-944965-32-7 (eBook)

# THE WELLSPRING

# Also by Lou Paduano

## The Greystone Saga

*Signs of Portents*

*Tales from Portents*

*The Medusa Coin*

*Pathways in the Dark*

*A Circle of Shadows*

## Greystone-in-Training

*Hammer and Anvil*

*The Gifts of Kali*

*The Final Gauntlet*

## The DSA

### Season One

*The Clearing*

*Promethean*

*The Bridge*

*Spectral Advocate*

*Dark Impulses*

*Broken Loyalties*

*For Iris*

# CHAPTER ONE

They moved her twice in the last week. Ever since the Buffalo fiasco, April had not called a single location home for more than a month. Lately, however, they pulled her from one spot to the next at any given moment. If the weather turned a certain way, she thought they might come for her — to take her to the next so-called safe house.

None of them were safe for April. They'd been designed by her, under the direction of others, so that her overseers were safe *from* her. The keypad, properly installed on an innocuous-enough building, allowed the space to be retrofitted to suit her needs and those working in the complex. Then, when uproot-ed — as seemed to be the case of late — the keypad was simply removed and the place reverted to its non-essential state.

April had called it practical beyond measure. They deemed it necessary for her protection. It was yet another lie on top of the decades of statements made by politicians and businessmen. The lock provided them access to April from any point on the map. All her equipment, and all her technology, was within their grasp to be mass-produced depending on their quarterly projec-tions.

When they came for her this time, she realized something had changed. Moving was a hassle. It slowed the timetable. It delayed progress on every conceivable level, and it disrupted what little sleep she was allowed because of the nature of her work.

"We're leaving?" April asked as the soldiers escorted her from the home in a quiet neighborhood north of Chester, Ver-mont. The sound of crickets filled the air. "What happened this time?"

"Doesn't matter," one soldier declared. His name was Oscar Valdez, though he preferred Oz. She knew this, but never let on the level of information she kept on her captors. It only ever upset them, and she didn't need any more drama. "We're heading out. Get in the transport."

"Can't believe we're doing this again," the other grumbled. Stephen Keller was a squirrelly little kid compared to the senior officer. April had seen him on more than one occasion torturing the rats in the lab for the fun of it. "How do they keep finding us?"

"Shut the hell up and get inside," Oscar snapped. He held tight to his automatic rifle, prodding her along with his free hand. "New safe house is being set up as we speak."

"Hopefully it's a room with a view this time," she remarked.

"Not likely."

They rounded the transport for the back. April could never occupy the cab with the soldiers. If they had their way, she would never be seen, merely smuggled from place to place wearing a hood over her head. They hated the sight of her. The problem came from more than ageism, though her elderly status came with its own concerns. No, the truth was, her very presence inspired nothing but fear and doubt.

Their fear came from ignorance—one perpetuated by her overseers. Few realized who she really was, or what role she played in the operation. They only knew of her vital nature to the project, and that she was to be protected at all costs. Liking her went above and beyond the call of duty. None of them ever even asked her for a name.

The second they reached the back of the transport, Oscar fell. The shot was silent, a puff of air that escaped on the wind. With little more than a stumbling step, he dropped to the pavement.

Stephen moved for him, turning him over on his back. The bullet had pierced his neck, and he bled out instantly. "What the—"

Another shot ended the man's question. Stephen collapsed over the corpse of his superior.

A figure stepped out of the shadows. He wore black from head to toe, including a mask that kept all but his striking green eyes covered. "Are you okay?"

"You just killed my escort."

"Your guards, you mean."

April cocked an eyebrow. "Somehow, I don't think your intentions are any better."

"You'd be wrong," he said. He held out his hand. "I'm getting you out of here."

He grabbed her by the wrist and ushered her down the block. Their pace started briskly, but her steps could not keep up. Her bones didn't work that way anymore, weighing her down more than ably assisting their departure from the scene. The masked man recognized the old woman's discomfort and slowed to a point, but never stopped completely until the safe house was out of sight. When they reached his car three blocks out, she pulled away.

"That's about far enough."

"I'm trying to help you," he said. "We have to keep moving."

"Not we," April replied. "You're going to let me go."

"What?" the masked figure exclaimed. "Not a chance."

"Then you're no better than those two," she said, hitching her thumb back the way they came.

"I..." he paused, unsure what to say. He ran his hand over his head, an instinctual movement he stopped once he realized he couldn't reach his hair. His hand shifted to his pocket for a set of keys. "Fine. Here."

It was her turn to be surprised. "What are you doing?"

"We can't stay out in the open." The man glanced around the street. "More soldiers will be en route when you don't make your rendezvous. I can't be seen here and neither can you. If you're not willing to come with me, then this is the next best thing."

April took the keys in hand. "You know who I am?"

"I do."

"And you're still willing to let me leave?"

His green eyes offered a sincere and caring look. "If you'll take this as well."

He handed her a cell phone, a burner as the kids liked to say—or, so she imagined, considering she'd never had the pleasure of their company while locked away.

"What is this for?"

"Susan Metcalf has been looking for you for a long time."

"Susan…" The name conjured up a memory she hadn't thought of in years. "You work for her?"

"Of a sort," the man said. His grin showed even through the mask. "She's been trying to help you."

"I appreciate the effort," April said.

"You'll talk to her?" he asked. "Trust her?"

"Trust, I'm afraid, will take quite a bit more than I'm willing to give. But I will talk to her."

"Reach out when you're safe," her masked rescuer said. "Call and we'll be there."

She turned for the car and opened the door. "What about you?"

"I'll be fine. But where will you go?"

April slipped into the car and closed the door. Rolling down the window, she smiled at the man. "I have some ideas."

# CHAPTER TWO
## *Five Days Later*

She came to the small town in Maine for a reason. April sat in the corner booth of the Blue Hill Diner, a small out-of-the-way place on the outskirts of town. A thin strand of steam rose from the cup nestled between her hands. The warmth ran up her arms and filled her.

The waiter returned to top off the cup. She accepted the gift with a nod of gratitude. When he was done, he grabbed the empty pie plate from the table and took it back to the counter.

April could still feel the late-night dessert working its way down. It was one of her favorite treats, but the dish came at a cost. At seventy-six years old, everything came at a cost, but sugar was one of the worst offenders. She justified the slice of rhubarb by drinking decaf without the added flavor that came with her usual creamer — at least for the first cup.

At her age, justifications typically fell on deaf ears and were summarily ignored.

Outside, the night sky beamed brightly. Stars filled the darkness. They shined down on the suburban town. The view relaxed the sleepless visitor, who sipped at her coffee and stared at the quiet of nature outside the diner.

Others did the same — the usual crowd for this time of night, by all appearances. Customers were easily recognizable by the staff. They shared stories, and passed along the nightly gossip, ready for distribution from the workday. Once the conversation ended among them, they turned to the night for solace. Only one ignored them all, and she was the reason for April's visit.

*Madeline Greer.*

She sat at the opposite end of the diner. Her dinner remained untouched, along with the milkshake dripping from the side. Madeline hunched over the table and the schematics spread out across the surface. She pulled at her curly blonde hair, twirling her finger through thick strands as she bit her lower lip. Frustrated grunts slipped out, drawing the attention of those around her every once in a while, but mostly she remained separate from the world — lost in her work.

April beamed at the twenty-year-old's dedication. She shuffled to the edge of the booth. Collecting her coat, April slipped it on. With her coffee in hand, she made her way over to Madeline's table.

"Stupid piece of crap," the girl muttered. She folded up the blueprints into a massive pile and pulled them off the table.

"What do you call it?" April asked from the end of the booth.

"Huh?" Madeline turned, surprised by the new presence. She patted the schematics at her side. "This? It's nothing. You wouldn't understand."

April set her coffee down and settled into the seat across from the young lady. She had a full view of the entire restaurant, including the front door and the street outside. Madeline gave her an irritated glare. While April took a sip from her drink, the young woman said nothing to rebuke her approach.

The cup returned to the table, and April clasped her hands together. "Well, dear, it looked to me like a dual-charge resonating battery cell."

Madeline's mouth fell open. She blinked rapidly to process the claim. "How did you know that?"

"Smart girl like you should know better than to judge appearances," April replied with a wry smirk. The young lady ran her hands through her hair, falling back against the worn cushion of her seat. April leaned closer. "You never answered my question, though. What do you call it?"

"The Infinity Cell," she said, chuckling as she did. "Stupid, I know. What I should call it is a failure."

"Why?"

Madeline jammed the blueprints into the front pocket of her backpack. "It doesn't work."

"It looked like it should."

Her eyebrows shot up. Curiosity, though, gave way to her

frustrations. "Yeah, well, tell it to my prototype." The large pocket to the rear of the pack opened, and Madeline pulled out a small device. "It's not much to look at."

She set the item between them. April hesitated, her hand open. "May I?"

Madeline nodded, and April took the device in hand. It was a mass of wires between twin battery cells. Though small, the apparatus was actually larger than it should have been to work out the kinks of the design.

"It should operate simply," Madeline explained. "Flip the switch and the second cell provides a continuous loop of self-sustaining energy for the first to draw on as needed."

April inspected the switch. A thin green wire ran between the two batteries. "Something is interfering between the pair."

"How did you know that?" Madeline grabbed for her milkshake and took a long drink through the plastic straw. "I mean, I barely figured that out."

"It's your casing," April said. She handed the device back to Madeline.

"It's all I had," she said. "The casing shouldn't be an issue."

"It is," April said. "What you need is a lattice casing to aid in oxygen processing. It will make the cell more efficient as well."

"That's..." Madeline paused. She lowered her project to the table, then ran her hand along her chin. "Hell, that's theoretical at this point. I read some studies about work being done at the University of Georgia. They haven't finished testing it. Where would I even—?"

April held up a finger, and Madeline fell silent. The older woman removed a small sample from her jacket pocket.

Madeline's eyes widened at the malleable yet durable material as it fell into her open hands. "Are you for real?"

"Your work is important, Madeline," April said. "Never compromise on your ideals. Tell me you won't."

"How do you know my name?"

"I want to hear you say it," April continued. Her hand took the young lady's and squeezed. "Please."

"I... I won't."

"Good," April said. "Now I need you to go sit at the corner booth on the far side of the room. Hide your gear in your bag. And do not look over here. Not once. Not even for a second. Do you understand?"

"What?" Madeline asked with concern. "Why?"

"It's very important you do this, Madeline."

The young lady took the rare and valuable sample and slipped it into her bag. The casing joined the prototype, as did her blueprints. Shuffling to the end of the booth, she strapped the bag tight over her shoulder. Then she grabbed her un- touched dinner and milkshake.

"Who are you?"

"Do it now, Madeline," April said, pointing for the booth across the diner. "Quick as you can."

She took a step, then turned back. "Thank you."

"You're very welcome. It was the least I could do after so many wasted years."

Madeline followed her instructions to the letter. She took a seat at the opposite end of the diner so that her back was to April. A stray glance shot her way. April refused to acknowledge her, sipping her beverage and staring out toward the front of the diner.

Lights flashed outside, the reds and blues of local law en- forcement. Mutters broke out among the patrons; inquisitive looks joined her stoic stare at the vehicles quickly lining the street.

Lowering her cup, April tugged at her left sleeve so that her coat fully covered her wrist. She clasped her hands before her and waited. She had been waiting for them ever since her es- cape.

Her time had finally run out when the bell rang on the door to the diner. Two men entered, one equipped with a sling over his right arm. There was hate in his eyes. The other stood tall and confident. He led the pair into the restaurant and directly to her booth.

She knew their names. She knew too much about the world, but when she saw them walk inside, their entire histories un- folded for her. Martin and Kanigher — agents for the NSA.

"You boys took your sweet time," she said as they loomed over her from the end of the booth. She offered the seat across from her with a smile. "Feel free to join me. I imagine we have much to discuss."

# CHAPTER THREE

Kanigher waited for Martin to squeeze into the booth before joining him. Grumbles escaped his partner; the pain of his injured arm made Martin more irritable than usual. Kanigher had tried to convince the man to step back from work after Martin's car accident the previous day, but he refused to listen. He had to be involved, especially after they finally located the woman they had been sent to find.

As soon as they sat, a waiter stepped over. He refilled the old lady's cup of coffee, to which she offered a satisfied smirk.

"Get you gentlemen anything?"

"Yeah," Martin started. "I need —"

"In a minute," Kanigher interrupted. Martin threw him a glare, which was promptly ignored until the waiter headed back to the counter.

"What the hell?"

"It's a minute, Martin," Kanigher replied. His partner was definitely more ill-tempered. It grated on the senior agent. "You can wait."

The bell on the front door rang. A pair of soldiers entered the diner and made their way over. Both were young men, struggling not to salute when they reached the booth.

"Local officers have secured the perimeter, sir," the lead announced. Kanigher hated having a detachment assigned to his team. He preferred people he knew to the strangers that had been requisitioned from General Adams for their operation. Kanigher's control over the mission, however, was limited.

"Good," Kanigher said. "Clear the place for us, please."

Martin held them up with a raised hand. "After you grab that pot of coffee on the counter and the biggest cup you can find."

Kanigher rubbed at his brow. "Painkiller's wearing off, Martin?"

A semi had struck the van Martin had been in less than twenty-four hours earlier. Martin walked away with a bruised collar bone, two busted ribs, and a broken arm. The three other agents in the vehicle weren't so lucky.

"Between that and the flight here," Martin said with a nod. He pulled out a bottle of pills and popped the lid. "You don't mind, do you, lady?"

"Not at all, young man." Her tone was cool and collected, nothing like Kanigher expected, considering the flashing lights outside or the armed presence in the diner. She held no fear of them. "You should consider the rhubarb pie as well. It's quite delicious."

"Come here often?" Kanigher asked. He took a moment to glance around the room. Her familiarity, her comfort in the diner, unsettled him. Had there been a connection between her and the other patrons? Had there been a specific reason for her to walk through the doors tonight?

One young woman at the far end glanced their way for a second before her eyes hit the ground. A soldier stopped in front of her table, his hand motioning for the exit. The woman stood, pack tight to her shoulder as she made her way to the front door. A sad look filled her eyes as they flitted in their direction.

"See anything, Kanigher?"

Kanigher watched the young blonde vacate the premises, then shifted deeper into the booth. "Nothing to worry about."

"You sure?" Martin said. "We can question them, see if they know anything?"

"No," he answered sharply. "I think we have everything we need already."

A cup of coffee arrived from the soldier. He passed it over to the waiting Martin, who took a swig. It dribbled from the man's chin. He tried to wipe it away with his right hand. The pain caused him to curse under his breath at his own idiocy.

Kanigher slipped from the booth and grabbed a napkin from the counter. While he was up, he reached into the glass display of desserts and removed a slice of rhubarb. He passed both over when he sat back down, then turned his focus to their guest.

"You know why we're here?"

She cradled her steaming cup close. "To keep an old woman up past her bedtime?"

"Cute," Martin said. "Real cute. How about we—"

"Martin," Kanigher said, cutting him off. He ran a hand through his dusty brown hair. When he caught the elderly woman staring at the act, he stopped and let the hand fall to the table. "I've got this. Drink your coffee. Eat your pie."

Martin took a sharp breath. He dug his fork into the pie. He bit into the crunchy crust; his eyes sparked wide from the taste.

"It's the sugar they use, I've been told," the old woman said. "Finest in the state."

"While we appreciate your knowledge of pies, we've come for information of a different sort," Kanigher said. "We know who you are."

"And I know who you are, Robert Kanigher. I know you very well."

Kanigher's eyes widened and his fingers tensed. He tried to ease up, but Martin read the concern.

His wounded colleague dropped his fork to the plate. "How does she know your name?"

The woman turned to him with a crooked grin. "The same way I know yours, Mr. Martin."

Kanigher cleared his throat. "This doesn't have to turn into a scene. We simply need you to come with us."

"I don't think so."

Martin pushed away his plate. He tried to stand, but his legs were locked in the booth. Instead, he leaned as if ready to grab the woman. "Lady, this isn't a negotiation. You are going to—"

"Eat your pie, Martin," Kanigher snapped. He caught the man's left arm and guided him back to the seat. He gnashed his teeth with each word, not caring for the man's quick temper or his lack of professionalism wherever they went. "The adults are talking."

"Use the napkin, dear," the woman added. "You look ridiculous." Martin grabbed the napkin and swiped at his lips. As he lowered it, she shook her head. "You missed some."

Martin took another stab at cleaning his face, dabbing at his lips and his cheeks.

"Nope," she said. "Still there."

Frustrated, Martin turned to Kanigher. He shifted close, his voice a whisper. "Did I... Did I get it?"

Kanigher sighed and rolled his eyes. "She's messing with you, Martin."

The woman laughed. "Most fun I've had in some time."

Martin crumpled up the napkin and tossed it aside. What little patience he had disappeared. Kanigher didn't need a repeat of recent performances. Hell, he didn't need any of the aggravation that had come with this operation. He just wanted it over.

"Changes are coming," he told the old woman across from him. He kept his tone civil and calm, which she appeared to appreciate as her laughter ended, and she settled in her seat to listen. "Changes for the group and for the way we operate in the world. No more sitting on the sidelines and hoping for the best. No more waiting to better people's lives. We need you to help make that happen."

"See?" The woman's finger wagged before her. "You need me. That's why you're not ready."

"Lady," Martin said. "This is happening."

Kanigher tried to calm his colleague down, but it was too late. Martin shook his head violently—unwilling to stay quiet any longer. "No, Bobby. I've heard enough. Now, you can either come with us willingly or not, but you're coming either way."

"Not."

"I'm sorry?" Martin said, shocked at the reply.

"You very well should be," the woman said, "but I sincerely doubt it. I've seen your use of my work and it saddens me. I don't think I'll be helping you again."

"That wasn't us," Kanigher clarified. "What we're asking you to do—"

"Will be the same. It always is, unfortunately." She reached for her left wrist. Under the sleeve, there appeared to be a tight band wrapped along her skin. At first glance, Kanigher believed it to be nothing more than a watch, but as she crept closer to the object, he noticed the metallic sheen of it.

"Ma'am?" he asked in a wary tone. "What are you—?"

Martin pointed to her wrist. "What the hell is that?"

"This?" She pulled back her sleeve. The band was attached to a small display. The screen came to life at her touch and the entire device began to hum and glow. "It's merely a quantum generator running off a watch battery. Haven't you ever seen one before? Quite marvelous, really. You just push this button on the side and—"

Kanigher jumped up, arms outstretched to grab the woman as she hit the button. "Don't you—"

The room filled with light. Martin screamed. Kanigher covered as best as he could, but it was too late. Blinded, both men waited for the light to dim. It was worse than a flash grenade. When the world normalized and focus returned to the blinded agents, they looked to their guest.

"What the hell?"

"She's gone!" Martin exclaimed.

Kanigher slipped from the booth and moved to the opposite side. There had to be some trace of her, some evidence left behind. No time had passed, so she couldn't have slipped out the back or the front. She had disappeared somehow.

"I see that she's gone, Martin."

"Did she vaporize? Tell me she didn't just vaporize herself."

Kanigher grimaced. "No. Your breath wasn't that bad. Come on, Martin, why would she? She obviously planned for this."

"And we didn't. Again." Martin rubbed at his neck. Then he lifted his broken arm. "I'm not calling him. After last time? No way am I calling Sullivan."

"I will, you baby," Kanigher said. He started for the door. "Let's go."

"What about my pie?"

Kanigher blinked at the man, who offered a sad puppy dog face next to his uneaten dessert. "I... I'm not even going to answer that."

He left Martin to make the decision. Stepping outside, the cold air whipped his hair in his face. Kanigher swiped the strands away, then retrieved his phone from his breast pocket and dialed. With every ring, he tried to find the right words to say—knowing there were none. His long night had just gotten longer.

"Sir? She's gone. The Wellspring is in the wind again."

# CHAPTER FOUR

Glass shattered, scattering along the inside of the clinic. Morgan Dunleavy swiped at the remaining shards of the small window on the door to clear her path. Unfurling her hand from the inside of her sleeve, she reached inside to click the lock.

No alarms sounded as the door opened. No lights flashed at her arrival to signal local law enforcement of the break-in. Instead, silence greeted her. She scrambled back to the green compact. Desperate hands slipped from the handle on the first attempt before successfully opening the door. All breath left her at the sight of Ben Riley on the back seat.

Blood caked to his skin and seeped from open wounds. Crimson ran in thin streams along the upholstery. His chest rose with short, shallow breaths. His cheeks paled; everything about him faded to a ghostly white—like he was being erased.

"Come on, Ben," Morgan muttered. She reached inside and pulled him to the edge of the seat before lifting him up. His arm draped over her shoulder, his feet dragged along the concrete, as she shuffled out of the rain and back into the shop.

She hadn't been sure of his chances when she found him in the abandoned school. He'd been shot and beaten severely—hunted because of their association with the DSA. Greg Sullivan had perpetrated a coup and was cleaning up loose ends.

Morgan barely survived her own encounter. Jacob Grissom, the man who had recruited her—who'd given her a second chance at life—had betrayed them. He had been serving the enemy all along, forcing her to question every choice since.

With Ben, however, everything was crystal clear. She had resisted him early on, his constant need for conversation bordering on inane. Over time, he won her over — through his deeds and his unwavering perseverance to do the right thing.

She couldn't lose him, not after he'd gone behind her back to protect her from harm. She wouldn't let him go that easily. Not until she got in the last word with him, at the very least.

The Blairwood Pet Clinic was a last resort. Morgan had noticed the shop a dozen times in her travels of downtown Bethesda. Had she ever considered owning a pet, it might have been a place she would have visited. Just the thought of a pet, though, made her laugh. Like her life wasn't complicated enough already.

The back room was little more than a supply closet. Cabinets of medications lined the right-hand wall. A double sink sat in the center of a counter to the left. Baskets hung on either side of the door, filled with combs, brushes and gloves, among other miscellaneous needs, depending on the day.

The cramped room opened to a narrow corridor. Three doors lined the left-hand wall. She stepped inside the first and saw the table within an examination room.

Carefully, Morgan lifted the dying man onto the table. Tremors shook Ben's body with each movement. She had no choice. The timer had been ticking down the moment she'd found him, and she sensed the end approaching rapidly.

"You hang on, Ben," she said. Her hand grazed his cheek and ran along his forehead. His fever was pronounced; heat coursed up her fingers at the merest touch. "I need you to hang on just a little longer for me. Please."

She raced back to the supply closet. Cabinets ripped open without a care and bottles crashed to the floor to find what she needed. She grabbed at scissors and gauze, forceps, water, and alcohol. Her panicked thoughts tried to hold a mental list, but it was shunted aside with each ragged breath of the man in the examination room. Morgan filled a basket and tore it from the wall before hurrying back to her patient.

The basket clattered at her side. Snatching a pair of scissors, Morgan set about cutting loose Ben's shirt. She peeled it back slowly to keep any pain to a minimum. There was no time for anesthetic, no time to even clean her instruments properly. Ben no longer had the luxury.

"No," Morgan said, struggling through her own jaded perspective. Ben was a fighter and had been fighting ever since she'd met him. He made her better by standing at her side. She could do no less for him now. "You can do this, Ben. We can do this."

The shirt pulled away to clear her view of the bullet wound along his right side. She pinched at the skin. Blood bubbled with each tweak. Lifting him for a look at his back, Morgan realized there was no exit wound.

"Dammit." She tossed the scissors back into the basket and retrieved the forceps. "The bullet is still in there, Ben. This… this isn't going to be pleasant. For either of us."

The forceps wavered in her grip. Her fingers tightened along the handle, but hesitated to act. She had left her medical career behind long ago, lost because of a choice she'd made. Three men had died to save the life of her brother. Nothing could make her want to live that moment again, to make those choices between life and death with the consequences that followed. The pressure was too much. Ben's condition, however, took all choice out of the matter.

She splashed alcohol on the instrument. Grabbing the pain-killers found in the supply room, Morgan force fed them to her patient to bring down his fever. Ben's arms and legs kicked out in violent spasms. Morgan did her best to lock him in position. Her hand rested on his chest. The soft beat of his heart comfort-ed her in no small degree, like he was in the room with her to guide her hand.

The forceps slipped inside the open wound. Blood clouded everything, but she did her best to navigate within. Every movement was cautious and deliberately so. Adding further damage to any vital organs would end the man's life in an in-stant.

Sweat ran in thick globs down her forehead and into her eyes. Her teeth dug into her lip, and her hand around the forceps tightened up instead of staying loose. Her body resisted her wishes with each rising doubt. This wasn't who she was any-more. She had failed in that endeavor like she would Ben and everyone else.

Then she felt metal. Eyes widened in surprise, and all doubt vanished in an instant. Digging deep, maneuvering through the thick blood streaming from the open wound, Morgan snatched the bullet with the forceps and pulled it free.

It clattered to the ground.

"I did it," she whispered, a smile on her lips. She dropped the tool in her grasp and reached for some hydrogen peroxide to disinfect the wound. "I did it, Ben. The bullet is out. I'm going to clean you up now. You have to do the rest, though. Come back to me, Ben."

Her deed, however, wasn't by any means a solution. Ben required more drugs to break the fever, as well as a transfusion from the blood loss. Both were out of her hands. All she could do was sew up the wound and cover it with gauze.

Finished, she wiped his brow with a towel. A sad smile grew upon her lips as she pictured Ben's reaction to everything she had done. He was always quick with a joke. Morgan imagined it would be about her ratty hair or the bags under her eyes. Something meant to be complimentary, yet at the same time completely inappropriate. She needed to hear that from him now.

Settling at his side, she continued to run her hand through his hair. "I... I don't have anything else to offer you but some damn prayers, and they've never been real good ones at that. Never worked for me. Not with my brother, my career, nothing. But you have them, partner, so you come back and stop being an ass about it."

"Morgan."

She fell back a step at the sound of her name. Optimism filled her at the prospect of where it came from, but quickly dissipated. Ben remained unconscious, dying before her. No, the name came from behind her from a shadow standing in the doorway.

Susan Metcalf waited with arms across her chest. She appeared soaked and exhausted. That happened when you spent hours burying the dead.

"How did you find us?" Morgan asked. The words were sharp with anger, something that always sparked with the woman who had been her boss.

"I followed you. I—" Metcalf stopped at the sight of Ben on the table. Her approach was hesitant, her hands falling to his side. "Is he—"

"I got the bullet out," Morgan said. "Stemmed the bleeding, but his fever is still spiking. He's dying."

Metcalf's hand fell on Morgan's. "There's nothing you can do for him now."

Morgan pulled away. Her eyes thinned. "I have to try. I have to do something." Morgan paced the length of the room, unable to look at the man who had wanted nothing more than her friendship — who wanted nothing more than to help people.

"You can," Metcalf said. "Morgan, I need you to do something for me."

Morgan stopped at the door. "What? What the hell are you talking about?"

"There's a reason why everything has happened today." Metcalf caught her thin gaze. "She's called The Wellspring, and I need you to find her."

# CHAPTER FIVE

"Are you out of your mind?" Morgan hooked her hand under Metcalf's arm and dragged her out of the examination room. Morgan pushed the former director into the supply room. Her side slammed against the counter. "I'm not leaving Ben."

The idea was ludicrous, to say the least. She had left the safety of Metcalf's self-proclaimed bunker to save Ben. Nothing would pull her away from that goal.

"There is nothing you can do for him," Metcalf said. "You said as much yourself."

"I… I can get him to a hospital," Morgan snapped. "He needs proper medical attention."

She couldn't though, or she would have immediately. The risk had been too great, especially considering the law had been the ones who'd inflicted such pain on the man in the first place. Morgan couldn't take the chance that more members of the new DSA Security Division were on the prowl for them under Sullivan's orders.

Metcalf knew the same, reading the concerned look on Morgan's face. "We're fugitives. They will arrest him and you will never see him again."

"I need to be here!" Morgan shouted. She squeezed Metcalf's arms. Her eyes flared and her vision blurred, wet from held-back tears. "I need to be here when he…"

*Dies.* She couldn't bring herself to say the word. Death was the only outcome left for Ben; his injuries were too debilitating, and his time too limited to survive any sort of transport.

Morgan let Metcalf go, and turned away from the frustrating woman. Her arms slipped tight to her body across her chest. She peered at the hallway and the waiting examination room. Her patient needed her, even if it was only as a voice in his ear.

Metcalf stopped her before she could take her first step. "There is more at stake here than one man's life."

The former director was gifted at bringing out the rage of those around her. Morgan was no exception. "Spoken like a coldhearted bitch. If this mission is so important to you, handle it yourself."

"I can't," Metcalf said. Morgan glared at her to force more from the woman. "Dammit, Morgan, listen to me. Sullivan has us by the throat. We're listed as traitors to our country. We have one advantage in this."

Morgan followed Metcalf's train of thought. "He thinks you're dead."

"Exactly. We can use that." Metcalf had been arrested early the previous morning by Sullivan's supporters. The transport responsible for delivering her to holding had been involved in an accident with a tractor trailer. Three men had died in the collision. Everyone believed Metcalf suffered the same fate.

The accident had been a ruse. Metcalf had set up the accident with her assistant, Stephanie Atwater, to fake her death. Falsified forensics corroborated the findings, giving Metcalf time to escape. Stephanie, unfortunately, didn't have that luxury. She had become just one more fallen soldier thanks to Sullivan's machinations—just like Ben Riley.

"How? What will you do?"

Metcalf leaned along the counter. The supply room door beat against the frame as a snap of wind pelted the edifice. "Set the record straight. Get us out of the crosshairs of every major law enforcement agency in the nation."

"Ben—"

"I will take care of him, Morgan," Metcalf said. She locked eyes with her. "I need you to trust me on this. For now, however, the Wellspring has to be your priority."

Metcalf's hand slipped into her pocket and removed a small note. She held it out. Morgan resisted taking the note at first. Her hands were clenched tight and her nails dug into her palms. Every word stung, as did the truth of the matter. She had done all she could for her patient. Prayers would either be answered or they wouldn't. Nothing could change the outcome.

Morgan let out an aggravated breath, then accepted the note. She looked over the scrawled location written in black on the torn sheet of loose-leaf. "Blue Hill?"

Metcalf nodded. "Maine. Leave now and you can be there by first light."

"And when I get there?"

"Support is in place at the coordinates."

That was it, the last word on the subject. Metcalf offered no details, no specifics of a plan. She merely tossed another agent at a situation and hoped for the best. She continued to hold back, even after everything.

"No," Morgan said with the shake of her head. She crumpled the note, then jammed it into her pocket. "That's not good enough."

"Morgan—"

"What the hell is this thing, Metcalf?" Morgan demanded. "What makes this Wellspring so important?"

"It's… complicated." Morgan waited for more. Her frustration caused Metcalf to sigh. "Fine. The Wellspring is the reason the DSA exists. At least, as far as my tenure is concerned. It started in snippets, fragments of information filtering through sister agencies. New tech, medications, innovations on a dozen levels being developed like clockwork. All by a handful of conglomerates. All under the auspices of a one-person research and development."

Morgan shook her head. Her hand moved for her brow, trying to focus on the truth behind the explanation. She could not fully grasp any of it. "What are you saying?"

"Vaccinations, cell phones, satellites, even military grade munitions have been fed to global companies by a single entity." Morgan nearly balked at the statement. Metcalf waved her down. "References to this are littered throughout history, and I've spent a decade of my life piecing her movements together for the sole purpose of finding out why."

"How? How could no one know about this?"

"Why would they?" Metcalf responded. "Do you question the vitamin your doctor prescribes or the microwave you use to heat your dinner? These are facts of life—developments we take for granted."

There had been many touchstones over the last few months

to corroborate Metcalf's theory. Yet all Morgan heard were Lincoln's words at the hospital in the aftermath of the Bellbrook affair.

"This is it, isn't it?" she asked, the words distant. "What Lincoln was asking me. What we're fighting for. It's her?"

Metcalf nodded. "It's the truth."

"They've been looking for this too, haven't they?" Morgan asked. "The Trust. And Grissom."

"Grissom?"

Morgan smirked. "Nice try, Metcalf. Like you didn't know."

"Morgan, I'm not following." Her blue eyes wavered. "What are you trying to say?"

"You..." She read her former superior's face. "You really don't know."

"What?"

"Grissom was working for them, for Sullivan or this Trust or whatever the hell you want to call them."

"He was manipulated," Metcalf replied. "They experimented on him. That wasn't our Grissom."

"Yes, it was, Susan!" Morgan exclaimed. "He told me everything. Every mission. Every objective. The Trust was behind it all. *They* manipulated us. He was in on it the entire time."

"No," Metcalf said, the word barely a whisper under her breath. "That can't be true. He wouldn't—"

The once-proud director staggered. Her hands fell to the counter for support. Morgan moved for her, then paused, hesitant to offer any sort of comfort. Too much anger remained between them and too many secrets. Metcalf deserved the betrayal on some level, or at least to feel it for herself the same way Morgan had when Grissom confessed to her.

"He was working with them, Metcalf," Morgan said. "He betrayed us, killed Stephanie and God knows how many others, all because of this Wellspring. How many are you going to let die because of this damn thing?"

"You think I don't understand what this has cost me? All I have to do is look at the man lying in the next room for a reminder. My department—*my life*—was taken because of it."

"Why now? If you've been searching for so long, why is she only surfacing now?"

"They... the Trust," Metcalf said, pausing to avoid letting

Grissom's name slip into the conversation once more. Morgan had said her piece on the subject, and Metcalf would either accept or deny it. That was her choice to make in the end. What mattered now were answers and a way out of the mess Sullivan and the others had created for them. "They've been moving her from operation to operation for quite some time. Ben accidentally stumbled on one in Buffalo. It's thanks to him I was able to locate her."

Morgan shook her head, hands on her hips. "At the expense of his home and everyone he ever loved."

Neither needed the reminder of what Ben had paid thanks to his curiosity. He had stumbled on a case larger than what it seemed. Because of that, he was framed for a murder he never committed, the culprits still on the loose.

"I found her soon after with help," Metcalf continued. "She's been on the run ever since."

"I don't like this, Metcalf."

"I know," she said. "But this is our only shot at answers. The only way to justify everything that's happened to us. To make sense of it all."

Morgan fell silent. Her steps carried her away from the supply room and back to the examination room. Ben lay on the table. He struggled for breath, each one a painful reminder of the little time left to him. She had to make his sacrifice mean something, to make sense of everything she had lost over the years.

Metcalf joined her in the hall. "I'll take care of him, Morgan."

"See that you do." Morgan swiped at her eyes. Both understood the stakes. There was only one path forward. She turned for the exit and her borrowed car.

"Good luck," Metcalf called after her.

Morgan stopped at the exit, the wind wailing steadily as a storm approached. "We'll both need more than luck on our side for this, Metcalf." She stared through Metcalf, her thoughts lost on the man dying in the other room: her friend and her partner. "We'll need a damn miracle."

# CHAPTER SIX

She never told Morgan the whole truth. Metcalf realized it as the car left the back-alley entrance to the pet clinic. Wind whipped around the space furiously before Metcalf closed the door. She pushed back the growing storm as easily as she had the rising questions from her subordinate.

The truth was funny that way. It complicated matters, as it also brought them to light. To Metcalf, there were levels of truth. Only she required each piece of the puzzle about the Wellspring, and about how she found out about the mysterious woman. Then there was the rest of the story, including how she'd founded the DSA and the whole reason for its existence.

Secrets were necessary in her line of work. They always had been, but she held onto them too tightly. Metcalf allowed them to distance her from others. That divide had brought matters to a head. Now she was the one paying the price.

Grissom had been working for the Trust. The idea was almost too much to imagine, yet the moment she heard the words from Morgan, she knew them to be true. Suddenly, the Oliver Blake operation made sense. The secret objective Grissom had been searching for, the one that had caused his death, had come from his cohorts at the Trust. They killed him, then revived him, so she could put a bullet in his head.

She loved him with every piece of her soul. She would have done anything for him, and he'd lied straight to her face. For how long? How many years had she been nothing more than a puppet to Grissom and his brethren?

Frustration grew, swelling through her worse than any storm outside. Fists clenched, she lashed out at the clinic counter. She slapped supplies aside, batted boxes and medications away in a fit of anger she could no longer contain. She never trusted, never believed in anyone, more than Grissom. He turned out to be the absolute worst person to honor with that level of faith.

"Dammit!" She slammed her hands against the counter again and again to force her irritation away. It was over—done and in the past—yet her guilt threatened to consume her every thought.

A sound stirred her from her ruminations. A brief rattling brought her back to the hallway and the examination room. It was the bullet removed from Ben's side. The gleaming metal rolled into the corridor, stopping short of her foot.

She lifted the bloodied souvenir and held it before her. The bullet was so minuscule, yet so damaging. The bullet had brought low someone she couldn't imagine losing—not with so much left unsaid.

"Ben," she whispered as she entered the room. She dropped the bullet in the basket at his side. It clattered between instruments until coming to rest at the base.

Her hands grazed the edge of the table. They reached for the patient, struggling for breath, but refused to touch his pale skin. She couldn't bring herself to feel his presence physically, to fully realize the fever raging through his body.

This was her fault. She had brought Ben into the fold, recruited him to the DSA as a favor to his father so long ago. The offer had saved him from a prison sentence. By pulling him into her world, she had condemned him to death. Prison didn't look so bad to her, staring over the wounded agent.

It wasn't right. Ben had done nothing to deserve his fate. He had been a light to the agency since his arrival, though she was loath to admit such a thing to his face. His jokes, his pride in helping others, brought out the best in those around him. She had seen as much with Morgan over the last few months. Even Zac Modine admired the man, which said something to his character.

Ben deserved another chance, and a way out of the mess she had created through her lack of faith—through the secrets held from everyone. She needed to save him. To truly balance the scales with his father, Metcalf needed to bring Ben back.

The shadows tucked in the deep recesses of the room shifted. She caught them from the corner of her eye. Metcalf let out a long sigh. The rattling had not been an accident. The rolling bullet had merely been the method of alerting Metcalf to someone new to the room.

"If you can save him, do it already," Metcalf said to the shadows.

He stepped into the light, a hand to his glasses. The lenses hid his eyes, reflecting the dim overhead light of the examination room. A smirk settled on his lips as the man known as the Witness approached. "Hello, Susan."

"I need you to save him," she said.

"Susan, I—"

"No," she snapped. "No ominous warnings and no more games. You don't get to creep in the shadows anymore. You are going to save Ben's life. That's why you came, isn't it? To help me? To save him?"

"No," he replied. He circled the table, inspecting the dying man between them. "There is a way, of course, but to do so would—"

"Don't," Metcalf said. She shook her head, hands clasped tight to the sides of the table. "Don't finish that damn sentence."

"He's too far gone, Susan," the Witness said. "Yes, I have the means to revive the man, but those supplies are limited. If I save him, there will be a cost. A life lost down the line."

"How dare you?" Metcalf exclaimed. She removed the Sig Sauer 1911 Fastback from her side. Extending the weapon before her, she took aim at the man. "How dare you threaten me after everything I've done?"

The Witness raised his hands. He continued to circle Ben's body. When he reached the end of the barrel of her weapon, his hand fell along the cold metal. Gently, he lowered the gun.

"I speak only the truth of the situation. It was not meant as a threat," the Witness said, his words calm and rational when nothing about their situation seemed that way to her. "I can save Benjamin Riley. If I do, however, someone else *will* die. And he will hate you for it."

Metcalf's bleary gaze fell from the Witness to the victim on the table. Ben was dying, his breath more and more shallow with each passing moment. He had lost too much blood. Metcalf wiped at her eyes, then shook her head.

"I don't care," she said. She jammed her pistol away before pointing to her agent. She had promised Morgan she would help Ben, promised the man's father even more once upon a time. It was time to make good on those promises. "I need him back. No matter what the future holds."

# CHAPTER SEVEN

*Did I make the right choice?*

The question followed Zac with every mile traveled. The town car skirted along interstate highways and through population centers. Each sight was new to him, yet the past dogged any enjoyment of the journey.

So much had changed in the last day. His wife had kicked him out of the house. His colleagues, the DSA Field Team, had been accused of treason and hunted by the very organization they had served loyally—some for years. The department itself was under new management. All personnel were investigated thoroughly to test their loyalty.

Loyalty was what it was all about, after all. Lincoln MacKenzie had told him as much, right before his death. Zac had done nothing in the man's defense. He'd made no move to stop Sullivan from ending Lincoln's life. No words had come to sue for peace, no bold choice that set him apart from a blind follower.

In truth, a follower was all he had become. Afraid of any recourse against him, Zac sided with Sullivan, hoping to learn the truth. He couldn't believe the charges against the field team, yet the evidence piled against them to an alarming degree. Zac had no choice but to step away from those he called friends.

A better question came to mind: *When was the last time I made the right choice?*

He'd confessed his affair with Morgan to clear his conscience, while also reaffirming the love he shared with Claire. The tryst had been a mistake, and rather than try to hide his indiscretion, Zac had owned up to it. He lost his family as a result.

There was only the newly installed director to rely on now,

the man who sat across from him in the back of the car. Sullivan grumbled into his phone; the confidence displayed over the last few months melted behind mounting concerns.

Zac had more than a few of his own. At the arrival of the first car during their trek north, Zac said nothing. He merely continued to stare at the landscapes passing by in a blur of shadow and light. By the time they passed through Pennsylvania, they led a caravan to their destination. Army transports paired with unmarked vans. He could see armed individuals in each of them as they fell in line behind Sullivan's car. A simple procurement mission expanded into a multi-agency manhunt—all for one woman.

"Keep me informed," Sullivan barked through his cell phone before ending the call. He dropped the device into his lap. His hands clasped together and squeezed, forcing his anger through them. "Dammit."

"Bad news?" Zac asked as he continued to gaze out the window. Darkness filled the sky. Zac wondered if the dawn would ever come.

Sullivan's hands fell to his lap. He lifted the phone and ran his thumb along the screen. "The Wellspring is proving to be quite elusive to our team already on site."

He meant in Blue Hill, the location Zac had found thanks to a text message received by Metcalf from an unknown sender. Somehow, the former director had kept tabs on the Wellspring over the last few days, hoping to bring her in.

Now it was Sullivan's turn, and it wasn't going well. The notion failed to surprise Zac, considering what he had learned about the woman. According to Sullivan, the Wellspring stood as the cause of all human advancement—every technological innovation and medical triumph of the last century could be laid at her feet. She handed humanity the future, yet no one could tell him the why of it all.

What was the purpose behind her actions? Where was humanity *supposed* to be heading?

Zac bit his lip, trying to hold back the swell of questions growing with each thought. He failed. "I was hoping for more about her, sir."

Sullivan cocked an eyebrow, obviously irritated at the query. "Like what? Her measurements? Social security number? What would appease the great Zac Modine's curiosity and quiet the throbbing in my skull?"

Zac's shoulders slumped, and he sank deeper into the seat. He couldn't afford to push Sullivan's buttons, couldn't risk falling on the man's bad side. Part of his worry rested with the dead man left at the DSA warehouse. The greater concern lay with his wife and son. He stayed with Sullivan for *their* safety more than anything else. At least, that was what he kept telling himself.

He cleared his throat. "You mentioned her role in major achievements. The Manhattan Project. The microprocessor. If she's been giving us the technology that's built our economy for the last century, why are you after her now? Why not just let her keep doing it if it is benefiting us?"

"It's true," Sullivan replied, hand to his beard. It appeared shaggy, not the neatly trimmed, refined look he typically displayed. The night had been long for them all. "Everything you've touched on is absolutely accurate, which shows you how little we've scratched the surface. If she held the secret to fission, the keys to unlocking the celestial bodies of space and satellite technology, then what else has she kept from us?"

Zac remained silent to mull over the director's words, and another good question to add to his growing list.

Sullivan noted his intrigue and leaned closer. "There is so much pain in the world, so much suffering surrounding us every day, yet she does nothing to end it when clearly she carries the means. She offers us nothing more than scraps and I, for one, would like the entire meal if available."

Sullivan's argument was simple. He meant to share the woman's knowledge with the world, to spearhead what he believed would be his legacy. Yet, if humanity did nothing to deserve the achievements that had brought them to their present state, it was possible they simply didn't deserve such knowledge. Maybe they were nothing more than simple cave dwellers drawing on walls. Maybe that was where they should have stopped in their evolutionary process if not for some outside hand—if not for the Wellspring.

Sullivan would have heard none of that argument. Zac kept it to himself, as he had so many things since turning to the man's side. He limited his counsel for his own safety and that of his family, who he hoped to make it up to someday.

Zac snapped out of his musings at the sight of Sullivan grinning at him. "This is our chance, Zac. With the Wellspring's knowledge and the resources at our disposal, including the DSA, we can make a real difference for humanity. Starting today."

"What resources?"

Sullivan huffed. His arms crossed his chest. "More questions, Mr. Modine? Your lack of faith is troubling."

Zac shook his head, regretting the question immediately. "No. Nothing like that, sir. Just curiosity, as you said."

Zac tried to relax. He felt his cheeks burning, his terror almost palpable, at what his pushing might bring from someone who had taken a life mere hours earlier.

Sullivan looked him over as he settled in his seat. "I will show you, then. You'll be able to see for yourself the potential held by this woman and why the secrets should be ours." His tired eyes left Zac for the world outside. A glimmer of light ran along the horizon. "Yes. First you, then everyone else. A new day, Zac. Here's to a new day."

# CHAPTER EIGHT

When Donald Stallworth had bought the house in Hampstead two decades earlier, he believed it to be his palace. He had hosted dinner parties, work galas, campaign fundraisers for friends. Hundreds had filled the halls in the lavish manor, all with smiles on their faces and money in their wallets to pass along to the cause du jour.

Over time, the events had faded; the guests had departed, and what was once his palace to be seen by the world had become a last refuge. It was his sanctuary, the last hope for silence against the ever-encroaching din of the modern day. The second the gates clanged shut and the locks on the door secured, Stallworth always knew he was safe. He was finally home.

Only the place was empty. It had been more and more over the years. Stallworth's work hours had always been atrocious. The extra devotion to law enforcement made the palatial property a reality, not that his wife ever asked for any of the extravagance that came with their lives once he was promoted to Assistant Director of the NSA.

She never cared for the galas or the fundraisers. She had wanted children, and once they arrived, their two daughters became the center of her universe.

He had forgotten about his family's latest excursion from the home. His wife, Nadine, might not have enjoyed the lifestyle his position earned him, but she partook of the money for her love of traveling. She and the kids were currently touring Yellowstone before heading south for the Grand Canyon.

They had planned the trip for the whole family. Stallworth had made the usual promises—each one less inspired than the last. Work made his absence a certainty. Sullivan's plans made any desire to escape impossible.

Usually Nadine merely put up with his absence, suffering in silence. Lately, however, there had been fights over the distance. She blamed work, though Stallworth recognized the anger behind every word, and understood it to be much more than that.

He had forgotten to shred the receipts in his pockets. He had found them on the dresser one night: evidence of the motels visited late into the night. Nadine had always overlooked his vices in the past, his needs that went beyond the conventional. As long as he came home to her, as long as their family remained intact in some fashion, she believed everything to be all right.

Something had changed in her. Age caught up with her, and she wanted something more, it seemed. Love was not something he carried for her. Their marriage was more about practicality than emotion. He didn't need love involved. Stallworth knew what he truly wanted went beyond such petty emotions.

Everything had changed, though. Instead of staying the course, using his resources to secure his own future, he fell in with Greg Sullivan. The former congressman had been an asset in the past. He had helped Stallworth secure his position in the NSA hierarchy; he had even assisted the naïve agent in networking with the right people.

It was how Stallworth had met the Trust. When the position opened up at the Department of Special Assignments for a deputy director, there was no better applicant than the man who had helped Stallworth so long ago. How he regretted that decision now. Sullivan's ambitions always surpassed his own. It was what brought the consummate politician down the first time. Now, Sullivan's plans threatened to drown them both in a political quagmire.

The DSA was gone. Stallworth had watched the reports from his desk of the building's collapse. The media had yet to realize what was stationed within the warehouse, but it was only a matter of time. All their work had been meant to turn the DSA into a weapon, a precision instrument in the counter-intelligence world, while they lined their pockets with the profits of their discoveries.

The moment the news came out about the explosion in downtown Bethesda, Stallworth snuck out of his office for home. He needed to get away, to break from the constant stream of information. Yet it continued to follow him wherever he went.

His phone chirped at his side, the same sound left with each message. It was the third in the last hour, and all from the same source. None came from Sullivan, who had more than enough to explain with what happened to the warehouse that housed his department. No, these came from the Trust—specifically the man at the top: David Hollis.

The thought of the man's name forced Stallworth's jaw to clench and his teeth to grind. Hollis required a status update—a reasonable request—yet Stallworth took it to mean something more.

"He knows," Stallworth muttered. He left the confines of the foyer for the living room. Just off the entrance was his bar, a favorite setting for most nights when he made his way home. He opened the flask of bourbon and poured a splash, not caring about the small puddles left on the counter or the early hour. He lifted the glass, his jaw still clenched at the notification waiting on his phone. "Dammit, of course he knows. This was a mistake."

Stallworth swiped the message on the screen. He needed more time. What he really required was some word from Sullivan about the Wellspring. At least then they would have some leverage. At the moment, all they held was the burned-out husk of a compromised operation.

As he reached for another shot of bourbon, he suddenly felt a presence in the room. He lowered the glass slowly. His heart pounded in his chest. This was his home, his refuge. Four guards were stationed outside at all times. He had spent thousands on the top of the line security system to deter intruders.

He kept his back to the room. A thin layer of sweat formed across his forehead as he crept closer to the edge of the bar. A hand slipped underneath the counter where a Smith and Wesson was tucked out of sight.

"Who's there? Come out," he called to the shadows of the living room. He spun around, revolver in hand. "I'm armed."

The lamp in the corner clicked on, illuminating his guest. She sat, demure and confident, with one leg over the other. Her hands rested in her lap. In front of her was a small table, on top of which lay the bullets to his weapon.

"It's empty, Donald," Susan Metcalf announced. Her sharp blue eyes drilled through him. "Like your threats."

He nearly fell at the sight of her. Metcalf had been reported dead—the victim of a car accident on her way to a cold, dark cell. There had been an autopsy, a death certificate, everything to indicate the days of staring into those deep blue tides of terror were over.

"It can't be," Stallworth said. He shuffled closer to the light. His meaty paw swiped at the sweat thickening at his brow and wondered if it had been his first or tenth shot of bourbon. "You died."

Metcalf smirked. "Then you're in a lot more trouble than you thought."

She lifted a hand. The simple act caused him to flinch back. He cursed himself for the reaction, especially when she did nothing more than display the chair before her.

"Take a seat, Donald," she said. "It's time we put an end to things."

# CHAPTER NINE

A flash of light sparked along the ground. The light grew in an immense bubble, filling the alley on the outskirts of Blue Hill. In the center, a figure took shape, and out of the light stepped the woman who called herself April.

The experience caused her to lurch forward, staggering uncontrollably from the rift and onto the pavement. Her hand jutted out for support, and she grabbed hold of the brick wall at her side. Turning back to her arrival point, April watched the blue light fade from view, as if it had never been there. A small smirk grew, the only reaction she had the energy for at the moment.

The trip sapped everything out of her. What she didn't realize was what it also took from the modified watch on her wrist. The device sizzled, and the display cracked from the use. April quickly slipped the latch free. The watch crashed to the ground, where the device burst into flames.

It was a onetime escape. She was on her own now. Unfortunately, her legs fought against her, as did all her senses. She shuffled toward the end of the alley to find some cover in order to recuperate. Barely making it five steps, April slid down the brick of the wall and met the ground.

She needed a rest, just a short one, before continuing. The watch wasn't tested. There was always the chance that her life would end with its use, but she had been willing to risk death rather than face imprisonment again. She had spent far too long under the heel of others. Now that she had attained her freedom, she meant to keep it, no matter the cost.

April reached for the phone offered by her masked rescuer days earlier. The screen was cracked. When she tried to turn on the device, nothing happened. It had not survived the journey. The phone's loss took away her last means of escape.

Nonetheless, April found the trip worth the risks involved. For the look on Madeline's face alone, April knew that to be true. How could she have been blind for so long? She had spent decades guiding the world, handing them their future one spoonful at a time rather than whole hog. Had she truly believed herself to be the only innovator left in the world?

"Have I made the right choice?" she asked herself in the quiet of the alley. "Did I ever even have a choice?"

Madeline had shown her differently. The child had created her battery without guidance, without millions of dollars from a dozen corrupt conglomerates. Her work had been simple brilliance, sparked by a creative force April hadn't witnessed in ages.

That moment changed everything. From the Wellspring's function — feeding intel to her keepers — to her very outlook on humanity, she had served a single agenda her entire life. She had set about completing a task so humanity would reach her goals according to a specific timetable.

They didn't need her any longer.

The smirk grew into a smile. The thought warmed her heart as much as it pained her. She had been wrong for so long, yet knowing that and rectifying the situation brought her comfort.

April closed her eyes. *A few minutes.* That was all she needed. *Just a few minutes.*

Footsteps woke her. Scattered, coming from both ends of the alley, they rushed into view. April struggled to stand, the wall a permanent support. She cursed her weakness. The teleportation device had drained too much of her strength, and now it had stolen all the time gifted to her as well.

"Don't move another inch!" a voice yelled from the end of the alley. It was the brutish fool from the diner: Martin. He pointed his silly gun at her, confident in his power.

She turned in the opposite direction, hoping for a clear egress. Two more soldiers waited at the street. They trained their weapons on her.

"Don't push us, lady," Martin said, slow to approach.

*Maybe he isn't as dumb as he looks,* she thought. His concern was evident. He did not know what she hid beneath her coat, what other gadgets might be present on her person.

"Tone it down a little, Martin," Kanigher said. He followed his partner, trying to slow him from action. "We have her."

"You don't know that," Martin snapped. "The way she bolted before, we can't—"

"I think that had more to do with your winning personality," Kanigher said with a thin glare. She caught his warning and nodded; her hands rose slowly into the air. "That's it. Let's not make this any more difficult than it has to be."

"Yeah," Martin grumbled. "I'd hate to have to deck an old broad."

Kanigher's arm shot out to block Martin from approaching. "Really?"

"What? Like you weren't concerned about that?"

The soldiers moved in. Martin waited until they were closer before he holstered his sidearm. He reached for the pair of cuffs along his hip and tossed them to the closest soldier. The young man caught them deftly in mid-stride.

"Hold it," Kanigher said. They paused, curious stares passing between them. Martin's practically screamed for a response. "The cuffs won't be necessary, will they?"

April read his piercing green eyes, as well as the serious tone. Kanigher was trying his best to control the situation, a laughable effort considering his accomplices, but she respected him for it. She bowed her head, the fight lost before it began.

Kanigher offered a nod of appreciation. The young man at her back hooked his arm under hers; the other soldier flanked her on the left side. They escorted her to the street and the transports lining the curb.

"Good," Kanigher said. He nudged Martin forward, who bit his tongue. She was positive there was another dreadful comment from the brute waiting to be told. Somehow, Kanigher kept it under wraps with his stoicism. "We have an appointment to keep."

"And a future to change," Martin finished, with an air of superiority.

The future was all they wanted. They had come to lock her away once more, to steal what she knew for their own purposes. She couldn't let it happen again, not after realizing the truth behind her actions. The time had come for her to make her own

choice, to tread her own path.
    A path no one would see coming.

# CHAPTER TEN

Morgan arrived at Blue Hill as the sun crested over the tree line on the side of the interstate that had carried her across four states. Exhausted and in desperate need of a gallon of coffee, she passed the billboard welcoming her to the town. A larger-than-life cityscape was displayed at its center with smiling faces weathered from the years.

She felt the same. Glancing at the coordinates listed on Metcalf's note, Morgan continued past the sign for little more than a mile before finding a vacant rest stop on the side of the road. She pulled in, and the car puttered into a spot near the edge of the small embankment.

Morgan left the car behind to stretch her back. The compact was not built for someone of her stature. Her legs cursed each step to the sidewalk. Few vehicles passed by the stop. Even fewer looks passed her way so early in the morning. Everyone appeared to be bleary-eyed and lost, like her.

There was no sign of her so-called support, and no sign of her objective: the Wellspring. It was a ludicrous thought—a woman behind the major advancements of an entire civilization. For the past century, humanity had made incredible leaps in science and technology; they had visited the moon and journeyed to the depths of the ocean. Mysteries unraveled daily thanks to innovations that cropped up almost as frequently. None of which could be attributed to any scholar, any genius in their field, according to Metcalf. All stemmed from one woman somehow directing humanity along a single path.

"Bullshit."

That was the only word for it. Morgan viewed the world

practically. She saw the people around her strive. Some failed, but others succeeded. Medical science had only skimmed the surface of its potential. Cancer was rampant, but now Metcalf believed the Wellspring—one woman—might know how to cure it, but hadn't yet? Advancements were parsed out like prizes for good behavior?

*Not possible. Not in the least.*

It took the decision out of her hands. Having that safety net, that belief in someone lifting up people like a damn fairy god-mother, took away the spirit of their struggle. The Wellspring's existence took away free will and replaced it with a sick form of predestination that soured Morgan's spirit.

She almost hoped the woman stayed missing; she never wanted to face such a reality. Morgan wanted to go on her merry way, believing—hoping—that people held the key to their own fate.

Not that there was much of a chance at finding the Well-spring. Morgan paced the length of the rest stop. She found no sign of her support, the details of which had slipped Metcalf's mind.

She never should have left Ben. He was Morgan's responsi-bility, her friend and partner. It had been hours since she left. If Metcalf did nothing, not that much was possible for him, given his state, then he was already dead.

Morgan rubbed her eyes. She couldn't think about it, about any of it. Ever since their return to Bethesda, they had found themselves on the run. No rest was to be found, no relief from the constant threats chasing them. Her body ached for sleep, her mind a weary cacophony of guilt and rage.

A car screeched into the lot behind her. Tinted windows blocked the occupant from view. The gray sedan with obscured plates skirted to a halt parallel to the sidewalk and the passen-ger-side window rolled down.

"Hop in," the woman called from inside. She wore her hair down where it laid along her shoulders. Brown locks blocked the right side of her face, covering the thin glasses over her wide eyes. She looked small, even in the cramped confines of the se-dan.

"Adler?" Morgan said. Her hand hovered near her sidearm, the lone weapon she had brought for the drive.

Peering through the open window toward the back seat, she realized Alison Adler had her covered on that front—not only in weapons, of which she noticed spare rounds and twin automatic rifles, but also tech. Tablets and laptops sat side-by-side with earpieces for communication, flak jackets and more. "What are you doing here?"

Adler was nothing more than an assistant to Zac in Operational Support, as far as Morgan knew. They had only encountered each other a few times since her appointment to the role by Metcalf. She had seemed nice enough, friendly and happy to share a joke or two in passing, but beyond that, incapable of carrying out direct operations in the field.

"We need to move, Agent Dunleavy." Adler scanned the road as she waited. "We're too exposed here."

"How do I know you're—"

Adler spun back to face her. "Director Metcalf sent me, Morgan. I'm not a spy for Sullivan. I'm not here to do anything but help you, so please trust me."

There was little else to do. Adler was right. She was out in the open. Anyone could take a shot at them from multiple vantage points, including the road and the forest. They needed to get to cover and figure things out as quickly as possible.

"Fine," she muttered. Morgan hopped into the passenger seat. As soon as the door shut, Adler slammed on the gas, and they were back on the road among the traffic filtering through the area.

"Metcalf never mentioned you, Adler," Morgan said.

"She wouldn't," Adler said with a smirk. "It's not exactly her style to spill on the specifics."

"True. How long have you been—"

"A few hours," Adler said, cutting her off. She shook her head. "Sorry for interrupting. I've had way too much coffee. I'll try to rein it in. I left during Sullivan's coup yesterday. Metcalf sent me the info on Blue Hill, and I hit the road, Jack."

"She give you anything useful?" Morgan asked. So far, all she had was the name of a small town in the middle of nowhere and an objective with no way of putting the two together.

"I think we have a place to start." Adler reached into the back. Her car slid from the lane to the rumble strip on the outskirts. Horns blared and curses flew as traffic bypassed the swerving vehicle. Adler's attention returned, her hand clutched tight to what appeared to be a survey map of the town.

"What am I looking at?" Morgan asked, taking the print in hand.

"I stopped by the county offices to find out more about this place. Records, property lines, anything that might make sense to locate the Wellspring."

Morgan waited for more. Instead, Adler hit the turn signal; the car exited the highway for a single lane road near the coast. "Adler?" Morgan finally inquired, tired of the silence. "What did you find?"

"You'll see," she answered with a mischievous grin. The car left the comfort of the road for a dirt path. When they reached the tree line, the car came to a stop. Adler was out of the driver's side before Morgan could question their detour.

Adler gathered up her belongings in the back. She pulled out a backpack and stuffed her laptop and tablet within. Morgan circled the vehicle to assist and found the pair of rifles waiting for her to take when she arrived.

Supplies in hand, Adler led them deeper through the woods. Waves raged against the coast in the distance. "Come on."

"Where are we going?"

Adler's boots crunched along the frozen earth. Morgan hated the cold. Luckily, she had worn boots and a heavier-than-usual leather coat before leaving Metcalf's bunker the night before. She still struggled to maintain Adler's pace—or her enthusiasm.

Adler pointed ahead. "There are bluffs up and down the coastline. Large coves hidden by rocky shoals and deep inlets. Most are unoccupied except for the occasional lighthouse."

"Then why are we—"

"It's this way." They traveled in silence; the quiet aggravated Morgan with each step. She had been traveling all night. Every minute she was delayed from her mission was another minute away from Ben. No matter the outcome, he deserved her presence, yet here she was, hours away on a wild goose chase through the woods.

Morgan nearly bowled into Adler, who stopped at the peak of the bluff. The tree line opened up, and Morgan stood in awe of the coast. The waves beat against the shore, the sound eerily soothing.

"There." Adler directed Morgan's attention across the divide between bluffs to their northern neighbor. Trees dotted the surface. Only a single structure rested at the peak, with a small driveway leading to a larger lot at the base of the bluff. Military personnel rushed to and from the building, with more transports held up at a makeshift cordon down the way.

Morgan failed to understand. "Adler, I appreciate your presence on this. I never had a complaint when Metcalf brought you in as Zac's second. But this whole mess is slightly out of your wheelhouse. We're looking for a person. A civilian, by all estimates."

"The Wellspring," Adler said with a nod. "I'm aware."

"She wouldn't be here," Morgan continued. "This would be the last place—"

"She is, Morgan," Adler said. Her eyes fell to the cold earth. "Not by choice."

"I thought she was in the wind?"

"Direction shifted." Adler cocked her head to the military presence. "They found her."

"Why would they? Why would the military be involved in this?"

"That's what I was trying to tell you." Adler retrieved the survey map. "I tracked this installation through county records. Then I cross-referenced with members of the DOD. This place is off the books, but one name came up in my search. General Adams."

The same man involved in Bellbrook. Adams had burned all evidence of the town's existence because of his ignorance about the situation, despite her protests. She barely escaped his wrath the last time.

"Great," she whispered. "No partner. No backup. Just the two of us in a situation we know next to nothing about. How many hostiles are we looking at, how many more lives are at risk, and for what reason? I can think of ten more questions if you'd like to hear them."

Adler nodded in understanding. Then her hand fell on her chest. "Hey. You're not alone."

"Adler, this isn't—"

"Oh," she said. "Not me. I mean, yes, you have me as well. But, well, we have a man on the inside."

Adler sat on the ground and opened her bag. She pulled out her tablet and passed it over to Morgan, who eyed it curiously. Red lights ran along the multi-layered screen.

"Is this a tracker?"

"Better," Adler replied. "It's a map."

"Of what?" Morgan said in confusion. She peered over at the structure across the way. The building might have been big enough for a single room—possibly four or five men stationed within, but nothing else.

"It's a map of the bluff. Or what's *inside* the bluff."

It was impossible. The scanner showed multiple levels, yet nothing appeared disturbed on the surface. How could they hide such a place from view? Morgan glanced at Adler, who couldn't hide the grin across her face.

"Why are you smiling?"

Adler laughed. "It's like a crazy super-villain hideout. How cool is that?"

"Not my word for it, Adler." Morgan crouched low to the ground and eyed the target carefully. If red dots meant opposition, then there was an army standing against them. "That is definitely not my word for it."

# CHAPTER ELEVEN

A security checkpoint greeted them at the edge of town. A series of bluffs ran along the coast beside them. Water slammed along the rocks on the shore down below. Zac had fallen silent during the trek. Every question irritated his superior, so rather than fall into the same trap repeatedly, Zac stayed quiet. He wrung his hands and tapped along his knees; Zac did everything possible to keep Sullivan happy as their drive went into yet another hour.

Two security guards surveyed the vehicle upon approach. One took the right side and the other the left in a sweep. They ran scanners beneath as they peered through the rolled down windows of the town car. Sullivan handed over his ID as they waited. When the soldier returned, he offered Sullivan not only the ID, but a salute.

Sullivan reciprocated, and the town car proceeded. They left the checkpoint behind and came out into an open lot at the edge of the bluff. It looped at the far end, a drop-off point that let them vacate the car in an orderly fashion. The other vehicles of their caravan parked in the lot. Multiple figures rushed to the transport trucks to open the containers.

Banners decorated the walkway; the American flag waved high above the rest in the wicked winter wind. Sullivan set the pace, and Zac was quick to follow. Others entered the line, though few spoke other than a welcome greeting to their neighbor or to complain about their back from the long trek north.

The entire place appeared strange to Zac. There was the pomp and pageantry of a military base — the security presence of one as well — yet there was no fenced-off complex on the site. At the peak of the bluff, there was nothing but a lone building. The single-story structure could not have been more than one thousand square feet in size from Zac's estimation.

The inside confirmed as much. A metal detector was positioned in the front of the room, a conveyor belt to the side that ran through several scanners being monitored by the soldiers next to it. Beyond that, there was only a single item in the room: an elevator.

"What the hell is this place?" Zac muttered. He had tried his best to remain silent, but the words slipped out and caught Sullivan's ear.

A smirk curled along Sullivan's lips as he led the pack to the elevator. "Patience, Zac. All good things, as they say."

Zac shuffled inside behind his boss. Others entered the car, shifting to the sides to give a pair of soldiers room at the front. The doors closed, and the car made its way down—*into* the bluff itself.

When the doors opened, Sullivan stepped out with his arms spread before him. "It's called the Cove."

Everything shined, from the walls to the metal grate flooring that ran in a long strip like an immense corridor. Stairwells occupied both ends; the steps ran down to more levels seen through the grating. Zac joined the others in their amazement, mouths agape at the sight of the place buried within the seemingly innocuous cliff.

He ran his hand along the walls. The sleek metal hid computer terminals every few feet, screens unlike any he had ever seen in languages he failed to recognize. "How?" he whispered. "I mean… this is…"

Sullivan nodded at the tech's excitement, unable to hide his own. "Ancient. Buried under rock until discovered by our people."

"Are you talking about alie—"

"No," the director said. His fingers grazed the writing on the wall. "The language used, while archaic and dead to our tongues, originated on this planet. *Humans* built this long ago. Impossibly long ago. Now it serves to usher us into a new age."

"Who?" Zac asked. "The DSA?"

Sullivan's laughter echoed in the cavernous complex. He guided Zac along the corridor past labs and work stations behind glass walls. "The DSA has, for all intents and purposes, served us as a tool, a resource, in searching out new technologies, new science. Now the two pieces must come together under one flag. Our flag."

Sullivan pointed ahead as one of his men posted a flier on the wall. It included an emblem Zac had only seen one time before: in Chicago during a murder investigation. In the image, Isaac Newton sat under a tree, an apple dangling precariously over him, a sign that knowledge came from the unlikeliest of sources. At least, that was how he imagined Reginald Kane felt when he'd met his end after seeing the mysterious logo.

The field team had been sent to investigate the murder. Their lead suspect had been Connor Hendricks, a man impersonating a federal agent. If what Sullivan was saying was true, had he been involved in Kane's death as well?

Zac's concern continued to grow with each step taken. Behind the pair, soldiers rushed into labs on multiple levels. They pulled scientists and technicians away from their stations. Others, less inclined to follow, were escorted at gunpoint and brought to rest on the second level.

"I don't understand," Zac said, trying not to pay attention to the situation below them. He peered through the glass into different labs for a better look at the tech inside. There were scanners that could pull apart a person's DNA and list the attributes associated with every genetic marker. Computer processors compiled information in a fraction of the time the current top models were capable of. "Sir, I don't understand any of this stuff. What are they working on here?"

Sullivan started down the stairs. He put his arm over Zac's shoulder and led the pair down the steps to the second level and the waiting crowd. "Little of late, I'm afraid. Advances are tedious and trying. The work slowed because of the Wellspring's absence. You see, while we labor, she hoards secrets. She holds us back when she should be pushing us to be better, to grow faster, and to reach farther. With her back in our possession, there will be no more secrets kept from us, including where this place originated and why."

*He didn't know. Did anyone?* How could a place like this exist unseen, with technology beyond anything Zac had ever dreamed?

"You said the DSA served a function for your group—a tool. How?"

"Zac," Sullivan intoned. "You've investigated everything from intuitive viruses to people with strange abilities. You, yourself, almost met your end at one with a talent for—what was it again—spontaneous combustion?"

"Henry Reed?" Zac said, confused. "He was a friend. He's being treated at one of our facilities."

"The Ark," Sullivan replied with a nod. "I'm aware." Sullivan stopped at the bottom of the steps and turned to cut off Zac. "Who do you think funds those facilities? Who makes all this possible?"

"The Inter-Agency Council—"

"Is a bureaucratic playground for the powerless," Sullivan said with a scoff. "No, I'm afraid the Trust has owned the DSA for far longer than you could imagine."

"The Trust?" Someone controlled the DSA, owned their agenda and their resources? That meant everything Zac had ever done was at the whim of some puppet-master fulfilling their own agenda instead of looking out for the betterment of the country or the world.

"Grissom understood that."

"Grissom?" Zac's voice was barely a whisper as he tried to piece together the information being provided. "What about him?"

Jacob Grissom had been the former Deputy Director prior to Sullivan's appointment to the role. He had met his end during an operation months earlier, looking into an unauthorized secondary objective. Zac had always assumed it had come from Metcalf. The truth was something far different. If it had come from the Trust, had Sullivan also played a part in the agent's death?

Sullivan smirked. "Nothing, Zac. He was just another tool. Like your friend, Mr. Reed. And like this place. With enough tools, we can rebuild the world. Especially the right tools."

Sullivan set his back to the tech and approached the crowd. The technicians and scientists onsite cowered in the middle of the corridor. Their hands were raised in defense as they rested their knees on the metal grating. Soldiers surrounded the group, their weapons at their sides but visible for all to see.

Zac reached out to Sullivan. "Sir? What are you doing?"

Sullivan jerked away, then clapped his hands to grab the crowd's attention. "Me? I am offering these fine people a choice." His voice thundered down the aisle and throughout the Cove. "Your former employers no longer cut your checks. The Trust is no longer in charge of this facility. I am."

An older gentleman stood, his brow furrowed. A soldier moved for him, but Sullivan waved him off to give the man room.

"Just who the hell are you?" the tech asked, finger leveled on Sullivan.

The director held out his hand to the soldier at his side. A weapon settled against his palm, and Sullivan turned it on the defiant scientist. Without hesitation, without so much as a sign of debate, Sullivan shot the man in the chest. He fell to the ground, clutching at his wound. His body spasmed along the grating for a moment, then settled, with eyes wide in terror as he died.

Sullivan lowered the gun. "You know exactly who I am, and now you know what I am willing to do. Renounce your allegiance to the Trust and serve a higher calling—a better cause for a brighter tomorrow. Or die."

# CHAPTER TWELVE

"You can't!" Zac jumped in front of Sullivan, blocking him from the group of scientists and technicians cringing on the deck. Most kept their gaze locked on the dead man slowly being carried off by soldiers. They tossed the man into the closest room and shut the door, not that it did much to deter the view for the group considering the glass walls lining the hall.

A few of the scientists stood. They quietly shuffled toward the soldiers, offering no resistance to the change in regime. When it came to a choice between life and death, survival was a pretty powerful motivator. The numbers, however, sparked nothing but anger in Sullivan's face. Zac could tell he had hoped for a simple transition, and those still on their knees gave him nothing but more targets.

"Listen to me, sir," Zac said. He tried to keep his voice calm, though his hands shook with fear. Zac had seen enough death over the last two days. Too many had fallen for Sullivan's cause—*their* cause. "There has to be another way."

Sullivan refused to look at him. He stared at the crowd, almost cataloging each man and woman, as well as their allegiances. Of the thirty staffers stationed in the complex upon their arrival, only six joined them. The others, disobedient in their silence, remained on their knees, with fingers interlaced behind their heads.

"There isn't," Sullivan said loud enough for all to hear. "The choice is theirs."

Zac shook his head. He stepped closer to the director. "Sir."

Sullivan lowered his gun. He handed it to the nearest soldier, who holstered the weapon without question. Sullivan grabbed

Zac's arm, then turned him around to look over the crowd.

"Choices have consequences, and we, as a species, have made far fewer than you would believe. That is thanks to *their* efforts, Zac. I cannot allow them to subvert where we go from here."

Zac failed to understand the man's meaning. They appeared to be nothing more than techs, grunt laborers working on the typical projects found in hundreds of facilities all over the world. What were they holding back from them? How had they impacted the world through their prior allegiances?

"So let them go," Zac replied. "Fire them. Send them packing. You can't mean to kill a bunch of innocents because you have trust issues."

Sullivan chuckled. "A wonderfully ironic turn of phrase, my naïve friend."

The man refused to waver in his resolve. Zac saw it in the faces of every soldier surrounding the group of civilians. They remained poised to fire, weapons aimed and locked on target. It was in the fear of the scientists and the technicians. They knew the cost of their insubordination—of standing for their principles over the threats from Sullivan and his cronies.

Zac needed Sullivan to listen, but had Sullivan ever listened to Zac? Their mutual respect had grown over the last few months. Ever since his arrival, Sullivan had made Zac feel like an integral part of the team—more than just a staffer at the beck and call of his superior, but a friend. Sullivan had shown concern where others ignored Zac. They'd fed him lies while Sullivan had offered him the truth.

Or so Zac had believed. Sullivan was different now: colder. Bitterness filled his every gaze, an anger at all those unwilling to acquiesce to his every whim. Had Zac done such a thing? Had he considered what Sullivan's agenda meant for him and the consequences of his actions? Lincoln MacKenzie was dead because of them, because Zac believed in Sullivan and the path ahead.

More death, however, was a betrayal of everything he had fought for since joining the DSA. The department was a place for truth, a place for an honest commitment to doing the right thing for others. Sullivan, himself, had argued for that very sentiment at one time.

Zac wasn't so sure anymore. He shoved away from Sullivan

and cut him off from the crowd once more. "You kill them and then what, sir? You kill anyone who disagrees with you? Anyone who makes a mistake while you achieve your vision of humanity's future? How do we better ourselves through those methods?"

"Call it necessary."

"I call it murder, sir!" Zac snapped. Any chance of a calm resolution left him. "It is nothing more than cold-blooded, uncaring slaughter. And it is far worse than anything Metcalf did as director."

Sullivan cleared his throat and fixed the collar of his shirt under his sweater. His cheeks flushed, but he remained stock still and upright. It didn't deter the young man.

"Please, sir," he said. He pointed to the kneeling targets. Some peered up from the grating at the man pleading their case. "Don't do this. It's wrong. Plain and simple as that."

The silence hung between them. Every single person on the deck waited for a sign from Sullivan. The soldiers awaited their orders, the scientists their deaths. Zac's body threatened to shake apart from the quiet that settled over them all. Sullivan's hand fell on Zac's shoulder, and a smile spread across his lips.

"You're right, Zac. It is."

Zac grinned in response; the breath that had been caught in his throat finally eased out of him in relief. His heart slowed in his chest, and calm returned to his body. He had never been one to defend others, never been able to articulate his point clearly when speaking out against his betters. That Sullivan had listened made Zac realize he had been right to come.

"Thank you, sir," he said, hand over his heart. "Thank—"

Sullivan held him up, a finger raised. Zac's brow furrowed as the director turned to the soldiers to the left and nodded.

"Sir?"

The order was given without a single word spoken. Merely a gesture was enough for everyone on the deck to understand. The scientists bowed their heads. The soldiers aimed at their targets and opened fire. It was over in a matter of seconds, though for Zac it lasted much longer. He heard each shot, each shout of panic and terror—the screams of the innocent and the desperate.

Then there was nothing.

Zac turned to see the fallen. Every last one of the scientists, unwilling to submit to Sullivan, had been slaughtered. They bled through the grating, and the dripping echoed in his mind.

The hand returned to his shoulder. Zac refused to turn, refused to face the man behind the murder of so many innocents. "It is wrong, Zac, but that's the world they've left us. I'm sure you understand."

*How?* It was the only question left to him. How had Zac not seen any of this coming? How had he not seen Sullivan for who he truly was?

"I..." Zac struggled for the words, afraid the next shot would be aimed at him.

Sullivan patted his shoulder. When his hand fell away, he leaned close, his lips inches from Zac's ear. "And Zac? Don't ever question me again."

# CHAPTER THIRTEEN

Sullivan held his head high as he strode down the gangway plank. The grating beneath his feet clanged with each step as he surveyed his new domain. He offered nods to the soldiers, quickly securing the Cove throughout the massive complex.

Deep breaths soothed his burning cheeks. With each footfall he heard the sounds of the gunshots which had ended the lives of two dozen men and women in service to the Trust. More bodies had been sacrificed for his cause.

He took them all in stride. They were necessary. The Wellspring was finally in hand, and with her, his legacy. That was all that mattered in the end. Every advancement and every innovation offered by the mysterious woman would be delivered to the population through him. The name Greg Sullivan would be remembered for all time as the man who changed the future of the world.

It should have been the proudest moment of his life. Instead, a deep pit sat in Sullivan's gut. Leaving the populated areas of the Cove behind, he ducked into an empty lab. With the door secured, Sullivan fell to his knees and clutched his chest. He fought for breath, struggled to calm his frayed nerves.

He released his chest and his hands slammed to the flooring. Over and over, he let out his rage on the metal grating. Curses rose from his lips. He had the Wellspring. He had the Cove and his allies within the Trust—his Newton Group—yet his dream slipped further and further away.

Nothing had really been secured.

When he closed his eyes, when the silence surrounded him, he witnessed the deaths of the scientists again. He had ordered their slaughter—no one else.

"Why?" he seethed. "Why didn't they fall in line? Why the hell couldn't they listen to reason?"

His was the right path. He wanted nothing more than to improve and enrich the lives of everyone, yet they had resisted. They sought to undercut his future achievements, sought to undermine his authority—the same as Zac had done in front of Sullivan's men. They all attempted to pull him down, to rip away his accomplishments… just like before.

Sullivan had been a servant to the country as a congressman decades earlier. One troubled meeting with a potential ally led to another. Prospective votes were handed out like party favors, all to win people over to his point of view down the line. Eventually, those votes came at a cost. Payoffs traded hands—all caught on camera for the American public to devour. Sullivan had lost it all in a moment of weakness. He had been betrayed on all sides.

He couldn't let that happen again. Yet he could see his plans unraveling before his eyes. The Cove might have been secured, but the DSA was buried in a mass of rubble.

The department was supposed to be his gateway into the intelligence community, to maintain his link to so many valuable resources. A means of protection, the DSA would have provided assurance to those wary of his coup.

Now the DSA was gone. His personnel, hundreds of analysts, had been detained for questioning in the bombing's wake. The incident brought the covert agency into the light. With every passing hour, more and more information leaked to the press. His main support had been ripped from him, forcing him to rely on other means to keep the Trust at bay.

That was what made the lack of support from the workers within the Cove so disheartening. There was no need for loyalty to an organization they only knew by name. The Trust had only been a title given to their overseers. No compensation had been offered for their services, no great pledge to their future or that which they attempted to create for the world. There should have been no delay, and no debate, at joining Sullivan's cause.

*Why couldn't they have seen that?*

Sullivan slowly stood. His knees creaked loudly as he lifted from the ground. Fists clenched tight to his sides, he took in deep breaths, hoping to settle the growing doubts. They were misplaced.

He still held the trump card: the Wellspring. Everything depended on her. She would prove to the Trust, to those who disparaged him during his political career, those who stood against him at every turn, that he had been right. As long as he had her contained and working toward his goals, there was no cause for concern.

Catching his reflection on the metal sheen of the table in the center of the lab, Sullivan wiped the exhaustion from his eyes. He forced every tired muscle to relax. Sullivan stood tall and proud as he straightened his sweater vest and centered his tie beneath.

His victory was at hand. He could not waver in his resolve. The world would change because of his actions and his place of prominence in the history books was all but assured.

Today was *his* day.

"Nothing can stop me now."

# CHAPTER FOURTEEN

"How dare you?" Stallworth barked from across the room. He stomped and raged for all he was worth, but with no effect on his company. Metcalf merely sank into the deep leather of the chair, comfortable in waiting for his ire to dwindle.

"You break into my home," he continued, "where my wife lives? Where my daughters play?"

His cheeks were a fiery red, his jowls bouncing with each verbal slap. Metcalf said nothing in response. She watched the explosive performance as she would a street artist, mystified at how easy it came to the man and how utterly false each outburst seemed.

Stallworth was a practiced politician. He served the security of the nation, but at his heart, he was always waiting to be called before the Capitol, where the cameras were the brightest and the entire world was his audience.

She almost wished she'd been recording his diatribe as he approached the corner of his immense living space. Slow steps acknowledged her request for him to join her. They carried him ever closer, despite the anger in his words.

"I could kill you, and no one would bat an eye. Not a soul would care for the passing of a black-hearted bitch like you," he spat with contempt.

He clearly loved the sound of his own voice. His sneer grew, but she recognized the truth behind his words. He was trying to remove the shakiness from his hands, his terror at her presence in the room. How she had managed to get past his defenses continued to confound him.

Security meant the world to him, and she had bypassed it

all—from the electronic lock on the gate of the estate to the front door bolts. They were easy to slip when you knew the codes and had a key, which she did. Nothing was outside her grasp, and with each vile insult thrown, Donald Stallworth realized it to be true. It didn't stop him, however. He needed the play of his anger to feel better about taking a seat and falling silent.

She glanced at her watch and rolled her finger for him to move it along. She had better things to do with her day.

Stallworth scoffed at the motion. "You don't have any idea, do you? The amount of power at my disposal? I wouldn't even have to pull the trigger on someone like you. One word, one single command, and security will be here in seconds. They don't ask questions. They know their place, where their loyalty lies."

Once upon a time, she understood the same. Metcalf had served the DSA and the country as a whole. Thanks to her dedication, she lost everything: her department, her love, and her life. Each betrayal stripped them all away from her. It took every ounce of restraint to not throttle Stallworth and his incessant tone. Because of him, she had lost Jacob Grissom.

*Grissom was working for them… He was in on it the entire time.*

Morgan's words haunted her. She wanted to stop the man's diatribe, wanted to demand an answer for her deceased love's motives. Had Jake really been working against her the entire time at the DSA? The very notion needed answering, but that was not why she had come to the palatial estate that morning. There were bigger issues for the living, and the dead had to stay buried in the past—at least for the moment.

Stallworth fell into the seat across from her. He unbuttoned his wrinkled suit jacket, and his gut filled his lap. "You should have just stayed dead," he snapped as he tried to get some level of comfort on the chair. "It would have been better for everyone."

Her hand left her lap and slid to her cheek. Her elbow propped her head up from the armrest. Still, she said nothing; she swallowed every unspoken allegation, every broken trust thanks to Stallworth and Sullivan.

The grumbling figure before her pointed furiously toward the door. "I'll call them, Susan. I will."

Each word faded, the anger little more than a whisper. Stallworth leaned forward, pressing for some ounce of fear in her eyes or twitch of her lips. She offered none.

Frustrated, he lashed out. He swiped the tabletop between them clean. The bullets from his revolver scattered across the floor.

"Damn you!" he shouted. "Say something!"

He fell into his seat, his chest heaving. Metcalf waited for him to settle. Then, with a smirk upon her lips, she reached into her pocket.

"No need," she said, the words cold and calculating. "I brought friends to speak for me."

A small thumb drive sat on her palm. She placed it in the center of the table. Stallworth stared at the plastic device. His fingers tightened against the armrests of his chair with every breath.

Metcalf pointed for the door. "But you go ahead and call your trigger-happy security. They might be interested in this as well."

He studied her for a weakness and found none. His was palpable, like the beating of his heart in his chest. The sweat along his brow took on a life of its own, like a thick film covering his skin. His cheeks were no longer rosy red, but darkened to the shade of blood fresh from the vein.

Stallworth grumbled and grabbed the laptop positioned at his side. It was exactly where Metcalf had left the device for him to use, knowing his curiosity would win out. He couldn't risk letting others in on his dirty little secrets.

The moment the laptop queued up, he inserted the drive. The display shifted to a massive file containing hundreds of images and documents. Stallworth recognized them all immediately without prompting.

Metcalf had done her homework. She had researched the man and noted every dirty deed over the years. When his eyes widened, she knew he had reached his late night trips with high-priced escorts and call girls. When he struggled to clear his throat, it was because of the bribes collected from state officials looking for help in hiding their own illicit acts. She had collected files from dozens of cases buried. Bank statements documented the payoffs to and from Stallworth's accounts—those hidden away from the public and his family.

Stallworth pored over them all until he couldn't take it any longer. He dropped the laptop on the table, then batted it away.

"Why?" he asked. His hands covered his face to wipe away

the sweat and grime. "Why couldn't you have stayed dead?"

"Too much to do." Metcalf removed the drive and slipped it back into her pocket. "It's over, Donald. You're finished."

"How?" he asked. "How could you possibly have known about any of it?"

"I keep tabs on my enemies," Metcalf said. "Same as you."

He listened to every word and read every mannerism. She couldn't help but let the smirk slip when she replied. He glanced at the blank screen on the laptop once more, and his gaze thinned. Stallworth sank deeper into his chair as the answer finally arrived.

"A mole," he said. "You crafty sociopath. You planted a mole in the NSA."

# CHAPTER FIFTEEN

The rifle fell flat against Morgan's back. She tightened the strap so that the weapon lay snug along her shoulder. Easy accessibility was a necessity in her opinion, but so was a desire to keep it out of her way. The Glock on her hip remained her first defense.

Extra clips slid into a gun belt that ran counter to the rifle strap—a precaution should she run into massive interference. She expected as much after her briefing with Adler, and after keeping a lookout of the military outpost at the peak of the bluff across the way.

"That's the third transport truck in the last hour," she muttered while holding tight to a pair of binoculars. The truck was unmarked, a plain white container. Its position in the lot obstructed her view of the cargo within.

Personnel had been her first concern, and they made up most of the deliveries to the hidden installation. A dozen men, most in military uniform, marched into the small structure, yet none returned. Their strange disappearance added credence to Adler's belief about an underground base built throughout the innocuous-looking bluff.

"There's plenty more on the way," Adler commented. She passed along her tablet, then joined Morgan to point out the information displayed. Morgan scanned through the page, but the information didn't make any sense to her. It was just code, the background intel of a web page the analyst had hacked. Adler read her confusion and snapped the page back into focus where Morgan noticed the false front which was being used. "I flagged this company weeks ago. They work in tech interests, including high-grade processors and servers."

"Why flag them?"

"General Adams' son is one of the chief investors in the project," Adler said, drawing a look of contempt from the agent. "Transports like this one have been making deliveries to this location all morning."

"What the hell is this place?" Morgan asked. The question grew more and more irritating to her. She hated the lack of information.

"From what I can read with my scanner, the surface level is nothing special," Adler said. She took the tablet in hand and paged through the diagnostics that had been running in the background since their arrival. Every moment gained her more access, thanks to their proximity to the structure. "For all I can tell, it might as well be a broom closet with an elevator to the main complex. But inside that cliff? I've never seen readings like these before. There are forms of radiation spiking that are unlike any on the planet."

"Radiation?" Morgan thought the place to be strictly military in nature. Soldiers were one thing. Adler was talking about civilians on site. "A lab of some kind?"

Adler nodded to confirm. "The biggest and most well-funded lab I've ever stalked."

"As if I wasn't worried before." Morgan sighed. She paced the length of the bluff and stared out over the ocean. Part of her wished the waves would pull her down, that they would take her away from all the fighting and the dying that surrounded every decision she had been forced to make of late. She never should have listened to Metcalf. This wasn't what she'd wanted.

Adler joined her. She held out what appeared to be a tiny ball with a speaker inside. "Here."

Morgan took the communication device and placed it in her right ear. She tapped it twice; the feedback spiked through Adler's own piece. A thumbs up confirmed the link.

"The radiation might make chatting a little tricky, but you holler and I'll—"

"You'll what, Adler? Come to my rescue?" Morgan snapped and immediately regretted the tone. Her eyes caught those of her colleague. "That's not going to happen."

Heroic deeds like that had earned Ben the bullet in his side.

He'd gone alone against Sullivan—a stupid and selfish act. It infuriated her. Her cheeks burned at the very thought, and her fists clenched tight against her sides. She beat along her thighs to put them aside.

Morgan had grown tired of others deciding her value, about the worth of her life over others. It failed to stop the concern in the back of her mind for her fallen partner. She could hear the wheezing of his breath and see the shallow rise of his chest every time she closed her eyes. Was he still fighting for life, or had he paid the ultimate price for his sacrifice?

"Agent Dunleavy?"

Adler waited for her at the supplies. The young woman who had led Morgan here offered a sullen gaze. She was out of her element to be sure, but required no chastising or rebuke. Adler had come out of a sense of duty, out of loyalty to what the DSA should have been and what Metcalf should have earned from all her subordinates, not the select few she deigned important.

"Forget it, Adler," she said with a wave. "And make it Morgan, all right?"

"Okay," Adler replied. She tucked a strand of hair behind her ear, then adjusted her glasses on her face.

Morgan slipped past her for the edge of the bluff. She raised the binoculars once more for a glimpse of her target. "Security looks impenetrable up top. I take it you've found me an alternate point of entry?"

"I have," Adler said. She guided the binoculars lower along the side of the cliff. The trip stopped about two-thirds of the way down to the rocky shoal below. "It might be a tight squeeze, but there's a ventilation shaft."

Tight didn't begin to describe it. Even Adler might struggle to climb inside, and she was half the size of Morgan. Their options, however, were limited and growing more so by the second.

"Well, it's a good thing I'm packing light."

"I noticed a trail leading to the water below. You should be able to climb up for access without anyone even realizing."

"Let's hope you're right or this is going to be a short rescue mission," Morgan said. She started for the thin trail down to the shore and took her first step toward the unknown.

# CHAPTER SIXTEEN

Zac sat along the deck. He beat his head lightly like a drum along the glass at his back. It was the only visible room on the level. Unlike the rest that held labs throughout or individualized work stations, there was only a table and two chairs in the middle with filing cabinets along the side.

An administrative office from the setup, Zac wondered who the small space belonged to. Was it one of the turncoats who had switched sides to save their own skin? Or had the office belonged to one of the dead?

The sound of the gunshots echoed in his mind, and Zac slammed his head back to mute the memory. Nothing ever would. There was no coming back from what his unconvincing speech had wrought. He had tried so hard to win Sullivan over and failed in every regard.

*What the hell am I doing here? How could I have been so wrong about Sullivan?*

He truly believed the newly installed director was the right man for the job—that through his earnestness, the DSA would once again be a respectable place to work. No more secrets and lies. It was part of the reason he'd confessed his affair with his wife: to wipe the slate clean.

Lincoln, however, turned out to be the voice of reason through it all. It *was* all about loyalties now. Zac had chosen Sullivan, sided with him against Metcalf. Now, his former boss was dead and his current one was murdering people who disagreed with him. He couldn't afford another wrong move. No more chances were coming his way—or worse, for his family.

He had let them down: Claire and Alex, Morgan and Metcalf.

Zac had failed them all, just as he had with Sullivan for not wanting more blood on his hands. It was different, though, and felt like something that should have been said long before — long before Lincoln paid the price for Zac's inaction.

So many were dead. Would he be next? It was a selfish thought, but a relevant one. Zac's fingers dug into his temples. He tried to drive out the sound of the gunshots, Lincoln's last words, and every other regret of the last few days.

Down the hall, two NSA agents stood watch. They introduced themselves as Kanigher and Martin, though the latter said nothing of the sort, offering only a grunt and a nod at the tech during the exchange.

Black metal paneling replaced the glass of the walls seen throughout the complex. Each section contained computer terminals which appeared to be asleep. Six doors blocked entry into obscured rooms, though only one was completely shut. Zac realized what they were the second Sullivan had led him down to the lowest level of the Cove: prison cells.

The Wellspring was inside the one at the end. Though no one mentioned her by name, the fact that guards were required left little doubt in Zac's mind as to the cell's occupant. That scant trace of uncertainty dissipated the moment Sullivan stepped out of the room. In his anger, the current head of the DSA squeezed his fists before him, his eyes bulging from his head.

"Blast that woman!" he barked the second the door closed behind him. He kicked at the grating. "I won't have her stand in my way. Not now."

Sullivan turned toward Zac. His glare threatened to burn right through the seated tech. Then he wheeled back for the stairs. His steps stomped along the metal as he ascended.

Kanigher sighed. Martin rubbed at his neck. Their shared silence bordered on awkward until the taller of the pair broke it. "Go with him." Kanigher hitched his thumb for the stairs. "Try to calm him down."

"Why me?" Martin whined. He lifted his broken arm in defense.

Kanigher cocked his head to the quiet observer down the corridor. "Want to stay here with this one instead?"

Martin rolled his eyes. "Therapist for the boss or babysitter for his pet geek? Rock and a hard place, Bobby."

Kanigher prodded him toward the stairs. "Just make sure Sullivan doesn't need anything, then get back here."

"Worried about her?" Martin tilted his head at the cell.

"Aren't you?"

Martin didn't reply. No snide comment slipped from his lips as his steps carried him away from the cell. His silence was evidence enough of his answer.

Zac stared at the closed door in the hopes of a glimpse of the woman on the other side. She had been at the center of so much pain and death—an object desired by all. Now she was almost within reach, and with her, the answers they had all been seeking. Yet Zac remained silent, lost in thought.

Kanigher worked his way down the hall. He made a show of his patrol with his hand over his Glock. At every door, he stopped and looked inside. He passed Zac once on the way down, and again on his return trip. Before he started another pass, Kanigher paused at a small cooler at the base of the steps. He removed a bottle of water and carried it over for Zac.

"Here."

Zac wasn't sure what to say, how to act. Kanigher worked for the NSA and their liaison, Donald Stallworth. His presence here made no sense, yet he had been crucial in capturing the Wellspring.

"Take the damn thing," Kanigher said, before he dropped the bottle on Zac. Cold shot through his body—a soothing balm along his skin. "You could use it."

"Thanks."

Kanigher continued down the hall, not bothering to look back. "Don't mention it. We could all use a break, don't you think?"

He hadn't before, but the man was absolutely right. Twisting off the cap, Zac gulped down half the bottle. He hadn't had anything to eat or drink in hours. There had been little time to even think of such things. He couldn't help but wonder if anyone else had.

"What about her?" Zac asked, getting to his feet. He collected his laptop bag from the floor and strapped it over his shoulder.

"Who?"

"She might need something to drink as well." Zac pointed to the closed cell. "It's been hours."

Kanigher nodded toward the cooler. Zac made his way over to retrieve a fresh bottle. He dropped his laptop to the floor before starting for the door.

"Hold it," Kanigher called. He picked the bag up and handed it back to Zac.

"I thought—"

"I'm not going to watch your crap," Kanigher interrupted. His eyes shifted for the stairs, though no one was present. Quickly, he moved for the cell door and opened it with a swipe of his access card. "Just be careful in there."

Zac nodded and entered the cell. The door closed behind him, locking him in. He stopped at the sight of the elderly woman seated at the table. Her silvery-white hair was tightly cropped to the sides of her face. Wrinkles lined her cheeks, though her welcoming grin added a youthful glow to her. She didn't appear special, or even dangerous. She simply sat and waited for Zac to make the first move.

He held out the bottle of water. Realizing he had been staring for what he hoped was only a matter of seconds and not the minutes it felt like, Zac's gaze shot to the ground.

"I... I brought you some water," he said before taking a deep breath. He carried the bottle over and set it in front of her. Her smile brought one out of him, and he relaxed slightly.

"I appreciate that, young man," she said. A sharp twist removed the cap, and she took a long, satisfied sip from the bottle. She caught his stare. "That's not all you've brought me though, is it?"

Zac rubbed at his neck. "Well..."

She pointed to the chair next to her. "Sit. I could use the company."

He pulled the chair out, then rested his computer bag on the table. Sitting, he watched her take another long sip. The excess dribbled from her lips, which she wiped clean. When she finished, she lowered the bottle to the table, her hand still holding it tight.

"You're her," Zac said, his voice soft in the cramped space. "The Well—"

"Everyone keeps droning on about that," the woman said with a huff. "It's a title. A function. I don't go around calling your boss The Pompous Ass Bureaucrat, do I?" A loud chuckle escaped her. "Actually, I might. You get my meaning."

"I think I do."

She extended her hand. "April."

"I'm sorry?"

"My name," she said as her hand fell back to the table. "Well, not *my* name, but the one that belonged to this host."

"Host?"

She smiled at him. "You'll catch up, eventually. Most don't, but you? I think you'll get there in the end."

"Thanks. I think." Zac rubbed at his neck. "April what, exactly?"

"I would have thought you knew," she said with surprise. "You're part of their group, aren't you?"

"Group?" Zac shook his head. "What group?"

"The Newton Group," she answered. Her hand extended once more. "April Newton."

"I thought…"

"They think they're pretty clever hiding the true meaning behind Sir Isaac, but I'm afraid I'm the real prize of the group." April stared up at Zac, her hand still between them. "I didn't catch your name."

"Oh," Zac said in surprise. He smacked the side of his head playfully, then shook her waiting hand. "Right. It's Zac. Zac Modine."

He fell silent, his quiet stare washing over her. He couldn't help himself. This woman had been the object of so much fuss, but to look at her he believed her to be nothing more than someone's grandmother: normal and mundane, not world-shattering extraordinary.

April, clearly concerned with the silence, lifted the bottle once more. "Thank you for the water, Zac."

"Right." Zac shook his head and stood. He didn't know how to start, how to speak to her. Who was he to say anything in the first place? Zac moved for the door and paused with his hand inches from the frame. He whipped around to face her. "It's just… why?"

"Why what, dear?"

"Your role." Zac crept back to the table. "Helping us advance. Why? Why help us at all?"

"You're a smart boy, Zac," April replied. "There aren't many who ask that question when you're offering them millions upon millions of dollars in intellectual property."

"I suppose not." He held tight to the back of the chair. "Is there an answer, though? A real one? Sullivan believes he can change the future with what you know. Can he?"

She ran a hand over her brow. "Everyone is always so concerned with the future. Yet no one understands the choices of today make the next a certainty."

"What if the choice wasn't your own? What if *you* made the choice for us?"

Her smile widened. "Exactly."

Zac let go of the chair and paced in front of her. "This is about control? Predetermination versus freedom of choice?"

"To Gregory Sullivan, and the people he once worked for, the choice has been made," April answered. "I believed it to be the same for myself. Until I learned the truth."

"Which is?"

She leaned over the table, a gleam in her eyes. "I think there might be some fight left in humanity after all."

"Fight?" Zac asked. "Against what?"

"Fate," she said. "One you never thought possible."

"How do we stop it?" Zac took the seat once more. He didn't know how long he had, but something in her look spoke to him. Some force of will made him want to keep fighting for the right path and a way out of the mess he had made of his life. "You've been playing us for decades, pushing us in one direction. How do we even stand in the way of something like that?"

"How else?" April held out her hand and pointed to the computer. Zac hesitated for a moment, then pulled it out for her. She opened the device so that the screen booted up. The gleam returned to her eyes. "With an idea."

# CHAPTER SEVENTEEN

Ben woke to the sound of cars in the distance. His body stirred, yet he kept his eyes shut to the world. His dreams had been vivid nightmares of falling—weightless and adrift. He thought he had been lost. The voices surrounding him had been so clear, yet far away. Morgan had been by his side. He remembered hearing her in the dark.

*Stay with me. Stay…*

Where had he been trying to go? He didn't recall. Everything was strange, even the sound of Susan Metcalf hovering over him.

*Save him.*

She hadn't saved herself, though, had she? Metcalf was dead. Someone had told him about the accident. Someone had been after her, after them, and she couldn't escape.

How had he?

Ben's eyes snapped open. He jerked upright, the sheets of the bed tossed aside in the movement. It all came back to him in an instant. There had been a fight in the alley on the side of his apartment building. Agents of the DSA, his own organization—or so they claimed—had come to bring him in on charges of treason. They had been lied to by Greg Sullivan. Connor Hendricks had shown up.

"He killed them," he muttered to himself. The words were strained, his throat dry. A glass of water sat on the nightstand table, and he grabbed for it. His hands, shaking and awkward, nearly smacked the glass aside in his haste. He slowed and ran his fingers over the cool surface before lifting it to his lips.

It wasn't until he lowered the glass that he realized the table was not the one kept in his bedroom. Nor was the bed or any of the fixtures surrounding him. Naked feet hit the thin carpet and Ben started for the window. He pulled the curtain back slightly, cautious against what he might find on the other side.

The neon buzz of the motel sign fluttered at the edge of the street. Few vehicles were parked in the lot and none drove by. The traffic heard came from the highway in the distance.

"Where the hell am I?"

The last thing he remembered, the final memory clutched tight by his thoughts, was of collapsing in the classroom of the abandoned school. Hendricks had fallen, killed by a bullet to the head from Ben's gun in a last act of desperation.

He recalled nothing after that moment, after he fell in the confines of the school—only the sense of weightlessness and the darkness. Intermittent voices had chimed from the void. He'd recognized them, yet remembered nothing about his survival.

"Morgan?" Ben called out to the shadows of the room. Her voice had been present, begging and pleading for him to stay. The sound of metal clanging against the floor rang in his memory.

*The bullet.*

Hendricks had shot him along his right side. The blood seeping from the gaping wound had been dark in color and thick in texture. There was nothing he could have done, no way to stem the flow in time to do any good.

Ben shuffled across the room to the mirror hanging in the bathroom. He turned the light on; the brightness forced him to close his eyes for a moment. He wore no shirt. The shot across his arm—the one that had merely grazed him—was gone. Ben found no scraped flesh, no burn mark from the bullet: nothing to indicate his injuries ever happened.

Along his right side, a bandage covered the other bullet wound. Ben removed the covering carefully. He found no blood, and no stitches remained in his flesh. Only a small scar where the killing blow entered was present, and even that had shrunk from the size of a puncture mark to the smallest of dots on his skin.

Ben's eyes widened, part in surprise and the other in utmost delight. He had thought it was over, that his sacrifice play to save Morgan and the others had been just that: the end for him.

He had done it for the DSA, to keep the work going and bring the light he'd always sought back to the world. It was a lofty ideal, but was the only one that mattered to Ben for as long he could remember. To play that part, to make a difference no matter how minuscule in the grand scheme of things, had been the right choice.

But he survived. More than that, he felt better than ever. The bruising on his hands and knuckles from hanging on the ledge was gone. The scraped skin on his cheek from the shattered brick was no longer a concern. Every injury had vanished, with little to no trace of ever having been endured other than the memory locked in his brain.

"It's not possible," Ben whispered to the man in the mirror. He continued to paw at his flesh, to run his hands over old battle wounds and fresh ones, for some understanding of what had happened to him.

So lost in his investigation, Ben failed to notice when the door to the motel room opened. It wasn't until it settled back in the frame, the sound reverberating through the space, that he snapped away from the mirror.

"Morgan? That you?" Ben asked. He shook his head at the sight of himself—still standing and still alive somehow—then turned to exit the bathroom. "I don't know how you did it, but I'm glad you—"

He stopped at the sight of the man in his room. He wore a grin that sucked the joy from Ben's face in an instant. "Hello, Benjamin."

"You."

The Witness fixed his glasses to his face and nodded. "Indeed. We have much to discuss."

# CHAPTER EIGHTEEN

Ben screamed. He raced across the motel room, hands stretched out in front of him. Grabbing the Witness by the collar, Ben slammed him into the door.

All he saw was red. All he could think about were the lives lost in Bellbrook months earlier thanks to the man with the opaque spectacles. Seven thousand people had died, including the lead agent of his field team, Ruth Heller. The Witness had shown no remorse, no guilt over so much suffering.

The entire affair had been a test to him, an experiment. Throughout the event, the Witness had remained cold and detached, like it wasn't real. Ben hated him for what he had done. Now Ben added his own confusion about his healed body, his own suffering at the hands of his enemies, to the list of crimes committed by the Witness.

"What the hell did you do to me?" he shouted.

"I..." the Witness gasped, unable to speak. His skin darkened from a lack of oxygen. His hands beat against his attackers, desperate for relief. Light beamed from beneath his eyeglasses, the color shifting from white to a deep red for a brief second.

Ben relented. His hands stayed in place at the Witness' collar, but he relaxed his grip. The Witness sucked in air, struggling through a spat of coughs to gain some of his former composure.

"Answer me," Ben demanded. He didn't care about the man's pain, not after everything he had done. "What did you do to me?"

"I saved you," the Witness answered. The white light was back behind his glasses, dimmed by the lenses.

"You?" Ben spat. "Don't make me laugh."

"You were beaten and tortured. Shot twice. Yet here you stand. There is no joke here, Benjamin, only the truth."

He remembered it all—every blow, every shot. All had been healed miraculously. Mere hours had passed if the clock by the bed was to be believed. Not a trace of injury remained on his body, not a stiffness in his joints, or the hint of a fever during the recovery process.

Ben let go of the Witness and stepped away. He wanted nothing more than to beat the man into submission, to call the police and have him sent to prison for the rest of his life, but there was more to learn.

"How?"

The Witness, freed from his attacker, shifted around Ben for the far side of the room. He lifted his glasses closer to his face, avoiding eye contact as much as he could in the cramped space. "It doesn't matter."

"Of course it does," Ben replied. He grabbed the man's shoulder and spun him around. "Tell me."

The Witness shook his head. "Any answer I offer will only lead to more questions. None will remove your doubts about my earnestness. My treatment worked. Call it a miracle drug. Call it divine intervention, if it helps. The results are yours to see."

"Why?" Ben asked, unable to hold back the question. "You're a murderer, a sadist who wiped out thousands in Bellbrook. Why save me?"

The Witness turned away. His hands clasped behind his back, which arched proudly in his defiance.

His behavior irritated Ben to no end. He needed to hear the truth from the man himself. For months, they had hunted the Witness to bring him to justice for his crimes. Now, while they were on the run for false charges of treason, he cropped up like nothing had happened. As if all could be forgiven, the past forgotten, by a single act.

None of it made sense to Ben, who had questioned his role at the DSA since his recruitment. His queries only intensified when he thought back to their first meeting in the clearing on the edge of Bellbrook.

"You said there was a reason," Ben said. "A reason I was brought into the DSA, but you didn't say what it was. Metcalf told me about my father. Is he why I'm here?"

"No," the Witness said. "That might have been Susan's reasons for your recruitment, but never my own."

"Then what?"

"Everything has changed now, Benjamin. You had a role to play in what was to come. That has now been altered, thanks to the drug that saved your life."

"Then why save me? If it screwed up your so-called plans, not that I believe any of it for a damn second, why bother to bring me back?"

"It was not my choice to make," the Witness said, his words solemn and filled with sadness.

*Then who?* Ben thought. The admission was a curious one. Who would have reached out to the Witness of all people to intervene?

Morgan sprang to mind, and Ben dismissed the idea immediately. Her hatred of the man exceeded Ben's own. There was no justification for the loss of so many lives in Bellbrook, not for a simple experiment, and not for the devastation caused by a rogue signal that turned people into trees. She never would have trusted the Witness at his word.

But who else? Metcalf was dead, the news given to him by Hendricks' team. Lincoln was in the wind. The suspects dwindled.

"Susan is going to need you, Benjamin," the Witness said.

"She's—"

"Very much alive," he interrupted. "She asked for my assistance, and I did what was within my power. Because of that choice, she's going to need you more than ever to protect against what comes next."

"And what is that?" Ben said. "What am I supposed to protect her from?"

"The future."

# CHAPTER NINETEEN

The climb was endless. Morgan's fingers dug into the cold earth at the base of the bluff, pulling inch by inch toward the ventilation shaft. Her body ached, and her muscles strained from the effort. She wanted to surrender, to rest for an hour, a minute, even a second. Time stood against her, and she continued her ascent.

Every few meters, Morgan lost track of her destination. The grate covering the shaft failed to jut out from the cliff side, blending in with the dirt and rock along the surface. A glint of light in the form of a red laser pointer helped steer her toward her destination. It was all Adler could do from her position on the adjacent bluff and provided the proper motivation for Morgan to climb for all she was worth.

The light dropped away, and Morgan tucked close to the wall. If Adler could not maintain her position, it was most likely because of a patrol rounding the perimeter of the military station at the peak. They appeared to be infrequent and for good reason. To them, there was no way inside the hidden complex buried beneath the earth.

The second Adler's light returned, Morgan picked up the pace. Her feet propelled her forward; her hands clawed for any handhold to pull herself up to the grate. When she caught metal between her fingertips, she realized she had finally arrived at her destination.

Adler offered her a thumbs up before ducking back into the tree line. She didn't need to be visible for what came next, only close enough to maintain communication.

"Patrol is still on the far side, Morgan," she whispered

through the line. "You're clear for infiltration."

That wasn't exactly accurate. The grate, though mere metal mesh covering the shaft inside, was locked in multiple places and soldered to the pipe. Working her fingers to her belt, Morgan pulled loose a pair of metal clippers—another gift from Adler, who had been more prepared than either of them imagined. There was a reason Metcalf had selected the mousy young woman. Adler's keen attention to detail with logistics made her a true asset.

Morgan set to work, clipping away the wire from the pipe. She kept her pace quick, the first three pieces snapping effortlessly in a matter of seconds. As she reached for the fourth, her left foot gave way. Panicked, Morgan snatched the grating. The cut metal dug into her palm. A cry escaped her; curses rose in the wind and echoed across the canyon.

"Morgan? Everything all right?" Adler chirped through the comm.

"Fine," Morgan said with gritted teeth. Using her right hand for leverage—the wire cutter still gripped tight—Morgan wedged her left foot back into place. Slowly, she removed the wire stabbing through her palm. Blood ran in drips from the open wound, but little could be done for it at the moment.

"Patrol must have heard that, Morgan. They're circling around."

"Great," she muttered. She snipped the wire as quickly as she could. With each shift, she dug her foot in more. Halfway around the pipe, she stopped. "How much time?"

"Thirty seconds."

Morgan pushed the grate away from the pipe. It had been worn down from the weather over the years, more malleable that she would have thought considering the secret concealed inside the bluff. She was grateful for the luck—it had been a long time coming.

With the mesh released and the pipe exposed enough, Morgan snuck her way into the opening head first. She only hoped her luck would hold and that the patrol failed to note the grate jutting out from the once flat cliff side. There was no way for her to turn around in the shaft once inside.

"They see anything?" Morgan asked, still concerned.

"You're clear," Adler replied. "They're heading off."

"Good," she said, then began her trek deeper into the shaft.

Cramped wasn't close to describing the narrow tunnel. Her arms jammed into her chest and her legs could barely bend in the confines of the pipe. It was metal but, unlike a typical duct, inflexible. It appeared to be used to vent whatever experiments were being conducted within the structure. As long as none were currently in progress, she would be safe.

The journey went quickly. After only one bend, Morgan saw light at the end of the tunnel. She scurried with haste to the exit, and another grate blocked her way. She gripped the cool metal between her fingers—her left hand still pained with each movement—and removed the cover. Careful not to let it fall, the grate dangled beneath the pipe as Morgan slipped free from the confines to the floor below.

The pipe connected to an empty lab, used for removing dangerous fumes from the testing site. No one noticed her entry to the room from the corridor outside. Morgan tucked the grate out of sight, then moved for the door where several lab coats hung. She pulled the tallest one loose and slipped the fabric over her black fatigues and the gear she had brought with her.

At the door, Morgan paused. There were no expectations of what she would find on the other side. She had no scanner with bio-readings, no real intel on the operation being performed inside the secret compound. Tying her hair back in a single tail, Morgan took a series of calming breaths and opened the door.

Her eyes widened at the sight before her.

The place was immense, far larger than anything revealed by Adler and her scan of the cliff. Levels ran down as far as she could see. The grated walkways opened up the view to the entire place. Labs occupied every level, separated by glass instead of walled off from view. The processors they had spied being delivered were placed before giant computers unlike any she had seen.

"He was right," she said to herself as she stepped out into the secret installation. "He told me, but I couldn't imagine, couldn't believe it. Ben was right."

# CHAPTER TWENTY
## *Two Days Earlier*

The volume in the terminal at Miami International Airport forced Morgan to cover her ears in order to think straight. Their gate waited for them at the far end, the flight back to Bethesda still an hour away.

She'd picked up a new crime thriller to occupy her time, purchased with the change of clothes to dull the sewer stench that had infected the last set. She thumbed through the pages, lost in the traffic that seemed keen to bump her in every direction on her trek to the departure gate. It wasn't until she was halfway to her destination that she realized her partner was missing.

"Ben?" She wheeled around, causing collisions on either side as pedestrians found their way around the tall beacon of a woman. Morgan figured Ben would have been chewing her ear off until she begged him for a moment to savor a chapter in silence. It was how he enjoyed their time together, the constant chatter — that need to connect when even in the quiet they could still be with each other.

Heading back down the corridor, she noticed him standing before the big board of arrivals and departures. His hands were in his pockets, and he swayed back and forth on his heels, his gaze locked on the shifting information displayed.

"Hey." Morgan sidled up to him. "What's wrong?"

He remained silent, lost in thought. Her words were lost in the surrounding noise. Ben continued to watch the ticking clock and the upcoming departures for the terminal. Buffalo ran through the list several times, final boarding being called at the opposite end.

Her hand fell on his shoulder. "Miss it?"

Ben offered a sad smile. "Like you wouldn't believe."

He never talked about it. Even when they were in Buffalo, his feelings about the place rarely found their way into the conversation. Sure, there was the whole rage virus that had infected him, and his desire to throttle Morgan to death. That may have cut down on the touchy-feely talking points. Nevertheless, she was surprised at how reserved Ben had been about his situation.

She pointed to their gate number, their departure still far off. "We have some time."

"It's all right, Morgan," Ben replied. He picked at his tourist trap t-shirt. "I know talking makes you about as uncomfortable as I feel right now."

"I'm offering, partner," she said, pulling him along the corridor. "Now spill."

"What do you want to know?"

"Tell me what happened."

He told her everything—starting with his routine patrol with his former partner. She heard the longing in his voice when he uttered her name, Emily Wright. For all Morgan had shared with him, she'd never thought to ask about his life, his dreams and his loves. She had just found out about one of them.

Then he continued with the nightmare. He had chased a young man to a house on Wex Avenue. There had been a keypad on the door. With the right five-digit code, it allowed someone entry into not the two-story double, but a warehouse that expanded for miles.

In his rush, he'd barely scratched the surface of the place. The metal grating used for flooring had allowed him to see everything around him. From his vantage point, Ben had spied labs, prison cells, storage units, and technology leagues beyond anything imaginable—a treasure-trove for the taking.

Then it was gone. He had stepped out, and the door had closed. When he'd returned, it was only the two-story double. He had never learned the code, never found out what the house was or how it came to be. Because of his report on the location, because his curiosity had gotten the better of him, someone had taken notice.

They framed Ben for the murder of the young man he had chased into the home.

Morgan listened as best as she could. She found herself more and more agitated with each revelation. Ben lost everything in the court case that followed. Expert witnesses testified against him using evidence he had never seen, never touched, yet somehow contained his DNA.

He was sentenced to twenty-five years for a crime he had nothing to do with. All had been to keep the secret of that house on Wex, and to hide the truth.

"So yeah," Ben said when he was finished. "I miss my home, Morgan. I'd give anything to have it back."

Soon after, they called their flight number, and the pair headed back to Bethesda. The sorrow of his loss fell away, drowned by his love to smile and talk her ear off. Morgan never bothered with the crime thriller. Instead, she listened to Ben laugh and joined him for a time.

But her mind always returned to the house on Wex and the secrets he had uncovered, wondering what it all meant.

# CHAPTER TWENTY-ONE

Ben had been right. His every description, from the grates as floors to the intricate details about the labs, matched what Morgan saw before her. It was the same as the house on Wex.

Morgan ran her hand along the wall at her side. It was made of material unlike any she had encountered: not metal or plaster, but a synthetic warm to the touch. There were no ducts for heating or cooling. The material must have helped regulate the temperature somehow.

Writing marred the space between rooms. Little was in English, and she failed to come up with what other language it might have been. Nothing jumped out at her as familiar; the symbols and iconography displayed were completely alien to her.

"What is this place?" she muttered. Personnel scattered from deck to deck; soldiers accompanied most of them to their destinations. She was the only one walking alone and suddenly felt very conspicuous in her surroundings. Morgan hurried across the deck, peering into different labs for some sense of the work being accomplished in each.

At the end of the row was a door carrying the words GENETIC ENHANCEMENTS along the top. She ducked inside and closed the door behind her. Not that the glass helped her maintain her cover. Keeping her head low and her shoulders slumped was the best she could do.

She had her mission—to find the Wellspring. Yet the room drew her in, pulled at her for a closer look. Morgan set about scanning the space. Inside, she found a table in the center. An intricate scanner hung from the ceiling above the table. Morgan followed the trail of wires to the displays along the far wall. On each were DNA encoders, gene splicers: theoretical instruments barely imagined, much less used daily.

Morgan worked through the operating system controlling the device. She immediately found a directory of subjects listed, each given a folder for different enhancements. She passed one named ENGERS and stopped at the one below.

GRISSOM.

*This was where they changed him.*

Opening the directory, Morgan tracked each document, and each test initiated on the man designated Asset Control Patient #330. It detached the technicians from their subjects—it dehumanized the process in the efforts of science and nothing more. The entire system was morally corrupt.

Morgan wanted to scream. She wanted to smash everything around her. They had ripped apart Grissom's life. The file listed everything. His exposure to the nanites in Oliver Blake's lab had made him the perfect subject. They knew the effects of the mad scientist's work, expanding upon it to enhance a new breed of controllable soldiers in the field. Those responsible had unleashed Grissom on her, had ultimately killed Stephanie Atwater and more by letting their subject out to play.

The revelation overwhelmed her. Grissom had given her a second chance. Even after his confession, she couldn't stop seeing him for the man she had wanted him to be. She swiped at swollen eyes, the need for further search unnecessary. Enough time had been wasted, and her objective was no closer to completion.

Her diversion came at a cost, though. As she reached for the door, a lab tech entered the room. He wore heavy gloves and a breathing unit, obscuring his face.

"Hey!" he cried upon seeing her. "You can't be in here!"

"My mistake," Morgan replied, hurrying for the corridor. He blocked her escape.

He ripped off his mask. "Director Sullivan asked me to clear this level. No one has authorization to be in here, so how did you—"

She decked him before he could finish his sentence. Her fist flew through the air and connected with his cheek. The tech crumpled from the blow.

Morgan rubbed her knuckles. "Couldn't just let me leave, could you?"

She ran out into the hall to put some distance between her and the unconscious lab tech. Her boots slid against the grating as she came to a halt. Two armed men waited for her.

"Don't even flinch," the shorter of the pair said. He wore a sling on his right side.

The other, taller and more built, looked her over cautiously. "Make the smart move here, Agent Dunleavy."

She read his icy stare and nodded. Slowly, she kneeled and raised her hands above her head. It was over.

# CHAPTER TWENTY-TWO

"What are you doing?"

The laptop was a godsend. April knew better than to refer to it in that manner, considering her creator. Still, there had been little in the way of progress on her part in escaping the Cove until the external piece of equipment found its way into her hands.

Zac waited patiently for a reasonable answer. She offered none with her silence. There wasn't time. Every computer, every system, held a backdoor. He was tech-minded, knew his way around an operating system or three, but remained clueless to her actions. The OS of the laptop guarded a secret layer of protocols, which were present in every computer on the planet. It was designed in that manner, a way to override everyone's access with the flip of a switch. The home screen faded to black. Coding language filtered in deep reds before them.

"April?" Zac said, shifting closer for a better view. "That language... it matches the walls of this place. It's unlike any I've ever seen before."

"It's old, Zac," April replied as she typed away at the screen. Each command layered against the system. All required precise instructions in the proper sequence to fall within compliance of the protocols set up ages ago. "Far older than this structure or the plan set in motion for it, for us, for everyone."

"That's not an answer."

April stopped her typing. She turned to her companion with a sad smirk on her face. "No. I suppose it isn't."

"Does Sullivan know?" Zac pressed. "About what this place is supposed to be? About what any of this is all about?"

"He never bothered to ask," April said. For Gregory Sullivan, it had been all about wants and desires — setting the future to his tune, for his legacy. Nothing had been asked about the why behind it all, nothing about where humanity was heading and what came next. He hadn't cared about the nightmares to come or the light to follow, should they be so lucky to reach it. "He's not like you, Zac. Sullivan is like everyone else who walked into this room — thinking of tomorrow instead of the moment. Both hold meaning, both are vital, but are rarely viewed in tandem."

April stood and moved for the back wall. She ran her fingers over the terminals embedded in the paneling. Everything in the Cove was accessible from each individual panel — environmentals, lights, power. The only thing needed was the access key. Unlocking the terminal, April released a twin set of cables underneath and pulled them toward the table and her waiting laptop.

Zac watched quietly, though his nerves showed in the sweat dotting his temples and running from the back of his neck.

"You're worried," she said as she returned to her chair with the cables in tow. Both were capped with USB adapters, and she inserted them on the left-hand side of the laptop. "You shouldn't be so worried all the time. It ages you."

"Why do you care?" Zac asked. When she sat to continue her typing, his hand fell over hers. "Stop. I need to know. I need an answer. Why bother standing up to Sullivan, to any of them, now?"

April leaned back against her chair. Zac's hand fell away, a sullen look of apology at his action. It was unnecessary, but caused her to smile.

"I saw it on the face of a young lady," April started, remembering her escape. She had journeyed east for the coast, drawn back to Maine. For what reason she couldn't say, until during a late night walk she had found herself on a college campus just outside Blue Hill. "She was alone doing some lab work not far from here. She must have been working for hours, covered in sweat and grease, unable to tear her eyes from her design."

April paused, then leaned closer to Zac. "*Her* design. One she came up with on her own, outside the tendril reach of the Trust and their associates. She saw something in her work. Maybe the future. Maybe God. But that creation belonged to her and no one else.

"I think it was that exact moment I realized change was possible. To make a different choice. To make any choice, really."

Zac ran his hand through his hair. Sweat caused the strands to slick back in a thick wave. "That's why you came here. Why you let them bring you to this place."

"No. I had hoped to escape, to keep making a difference and subvert the work I had done all my life," April said. "Coming here was never what I wanted, but perhaps it was what I needed. A chance to help balance the scales."

April went back to the laptop. The commands were placed; the protocols typed in precisely. With access to the Cove's intricate processors established, there was only one last thing to do. She hit the ENTER key, and the screen went dark.

So did the lights above them.

"What?" Zac jerked upright and stood from his chair. The metal legs clattered to the ground. "What happened? What did you do?"

"I took away their power."

The door to her cell clicked open—the locks bypassed when the power reset. Red emergency lighting illuminated from the walls. Every computer screen from every terminal in the prison cell came to life. All displayed a single instruction: a countdown. It started at fifteen minutes; the clock chirped with each passing second.

"April—"

She disconnected the cables and threw them to the ground. The laptop snapped shut, and she shuffled the device back into the bag. Closing it up, she tossed the bag to Zac, who caught the strap awkwardly. He continued to stare at the countdown blinking behind her. April shook her head and pointed to the open door.

"We should go now."

# CHAPTER TWENTY-THREE

The man in the sling snickered under his breath. He circled her cautiously. Pulling off her stolen lab coat, he found the rifle strapped to her back, and the arsenal wrapped tight to her chest. He tucked his weapon away to strip her of her own defenses.

He enjoyed it far too much for her liking. Even with only one viable hand, Morgan felt his touch in all the wrong places. It wasn't until his partner cleared his throat that the man's focus returned to the armaments.

"And I thought this assignment wouldn't be fun," he said with a wry smile. He dropped the rifle; the weapon clattered along the grating. The wounded agent cursed his clumsiness, then continued to unlatch the gun belt she had strapped for emergencies.

"Martin, let me—"

"Agent Kanigher worries about me," Martin whispered in her ear.

"That's not—"

"Don't worry, Bobby. I've got this."

Morgan wanted to scream. She had been distracted thanks to finding the lab that had turned Grissom into a killing machine. That sort of oversight never would have happened had she not been so blasted tired.

She was running on fumes, her eyes barely able to see straight, not that she wanted to see the stained and chipped teeth of her captor, much less be on the same planet with a man like Martin.

"Finished?" Kanigher asked. His irritation fit with her own, but he kept his gun trained on her. He didn't give her an inch, not a second of relief for which to come up with a plan.

"Allow me this one little joy," Martin answered. His hand stripped her of her Glock, the last remaining weapon in her once proud arsenal. When he finally completed his thorough search—to which Morgan wanted nothing more than to snap the man's wrist—he moved beside his cohort. His pistol was back in his hand, staring her in the face. "I was hoping it would be your boss at the end of this barrel, but a truck took that away from me. I got lucky in the collision and luckier still to be able to take out every ounce of pain in my collar, every agony in my arm, every mind-numbing wince from my cracked teeth—all of it—on you."

He backhanded her across the face. The added weight of his gun caused her to fall to the ground. She immediately pushed herself back up. Blood ran from her lip, and she spit it to the floor.

*Dammit.* She thought they might take her to a cell, some area where they kept other prisoners. It was the only play left to her, the only way to find the Wellspring. But Martin wasn't taking her anywhere—not if he had his way. There was hate in the man's eyes. It surprised her, considering she had never met the pair before today.

Martin cackled at his dominance over her. Kanigher, however, remained reserved. He lowered his weapon. "We should bring her to Sullivan," the stoic agent said. "He should have some say in what we do with her."

"Come on, man," Martin said with a groan. He inched closer, his gun right in her face. "You should be with me on this. The grief we've endured. That whole mess with Riley? These DSA clowns have earned a quick finish in the garbage dump of history."

*That whole mess with Riley?* Now the man's frustration made sense. How her partner managed to piss off everyone around him astounded her, yet at the same time comforted her. She wished he was with her—knowing he was on some level the way Martin railed against him and the DSA.

"You with me, Bobby?" Martin said.

Kanigher remained silent. A sigh escaped his lips, his eyes never betraying his thoughts. He raised his Glock at her.

"That's my partner." Martin turned to Morgan, his lip curled.

Morgan waited and wished the end would come quietly or not at all. "Say hello to your boss for me, bitch."

She closed her eyes on reflex, or at least she thought she had. Every light in the complex went dark. The bright bulbs that ran through every corridor above, below, and along each wall went out at the same moment, drowning them in shadow.

"What the hell?" Martin said. "Something is always spoiling my fun."

Morgan tried to move, tried to shift away from him before his focus returned. It was too late, her mind as exhausted as the rest of her. Maybe it was for the best this way. Stephanie was gone. So was the DSA in any form that ever mattered to her. There had been too many lies, too many secrets kept to think it could work again. Her death might even the scales somehow from her ignorance over her entire career.

Emergency lighting kicked in. The same bright paneling offered a dim red that turned the world the color of blood. A fitting touch for the moment in her eyes, though they were locked on the barrel of Martin's gun. Martin, however, was no longer looking at her. He was staring down the barrel of Kanigher's Glock.

"Bobby?"

"I tried to find another way," Kanigher said. His eyes glistened under the red lights. "I tried to keep you out of it, but you pushed to be here and you pushed for this."

"She's the enemy!"

"No, old friend," he replied. "You are."

Martin spun his arm, taking the target off Morgan for a second. It was far too late. Kanigher pulled the trigger, and the echo filled the cavernous structure. The bullet caught Martin dead center in the chest. The agent collapsed to the floor. His gun slipped from his hand and crashed to the ground right in front of Morgan. She snatched it up and took aim at Kanigher, who continued to stare over the dead man at his feet.

She held the gun before her with both hands, shaking with anger and confusion. Kanigher lowered his Glock to his holster.

"Easy, Morgan, easy."

"What the hell did you do? Who the hell are you?" she exclaimed, afraid of the answer.

Kanigher reached out to her. "Susan asked me to lend you a hand. You look like you could use one."

# CHAPTER TWENTY-FOUR

Stallworth fell silent at the revelation. Metcalf waited patiently, letting the details fill in with everything the blubbery figure had learned during their discussion. She didn't have to argue and fight to move forward. She had him right where she wanted him.

The drive in her pocket contained everything she had accumulated over the years. The details of every backroom deal, and every late night tryst, were contained in photos and documents procured from Stallworth's own office. He had questioned none of them. They couldn't be disavowed, not to any convincing degree, and she was not the one who needed convincing. No, that would come later.

"How long?" he finally asked. His hand ran over his chin. He continued to work through the idea that a mole existed in his organization. It was arrogance—it always was, to some degree, for men in power—they always believed themselves to be untouchable. Stallworth's eyes widened. He had figured it out. "How long has Kanigher worked for you?"

A smile slipped from her lips. Robert Kanigher was one of Stallworth's trusted agents and had been for years. Looking back at the man's career, one would never have thought for a second he had a duplicitous bone in his body. He had served the NSA for the last nine years after a decorated career in the military. That was where she had met the man—when he was the partner of another trusted soul: Jacob Grissom.

It had been a lifetime ago. Or so they made it appear when she'd asked Kanigher to take a position with the National Security Agency.

"Since the beginning," Metcalf replied. "He came aboard after Grissom, but I found a better use for him than field agent for the DSA."

"Why?" Stallworth reached for the laptop and slammed the screen shut. "Recordings. Photos. You've been amassing evidence for years. Why wait until now?"

"I didn't see a need to use it," Metcalf said. "If I had known, I would have, believe me."

The truth was that she hadn't cared about Stallworth enough to act. She had always believed him to be a blowhard and morally corrupt, but he'd served a purpose. As long as he assisted with the function of the DSA, Metcalf felt no need to press the issue. Besides, who cared who the man had been sleeping with? The man's vices made little difference — until they did.

"If I had known what was coming, Donald, I would have watched you flush your career down the toilet with a smile on my face," Metcalf said. Her hands clasped tight in front of her. "And trust me, I will smile when your hearing before the Joint Chiefs is televised for the world to see."

"Never going to happen," Stallworth answered with a wave of his hand. Despite the sweat coating his skin and the terror in his eyes, the arrogance remained. "With one snap of my finger, this goes away."

Metcalf shook her head. "That may have been true at one time. But you broke with your puppet masters, didn't you? You cut your own strings without a prayer of a net beneath you."

The Trust. Their secrets were starting to spill out, like the fact that Stallworth and Sullivan were acting against the interests of their former masters. It was the only reason things had escalated against Metcalf and her team. People were dead, the DSA destroyed, all because of their headstrong desire for power. From everything she knew about the Trust, they never would have been so sloppy in their execution of a coup. She would have been dead, they all would have been dead, if it had been a sanctioned operation.

Stallworth pawed at his forehead. His bloodshot eyes flitted toward the front door of his lavish home, then back to his uninvited guest. "My men —"

"Have just been delivered the early edition of the Times, the Post, and the Journal," Metcalf said. She fought through the anger in her voice, the rage at the loss of so much so quickly. Neither was required. She ran her tongue over her teeth, a calm washing over her. "You weren't my first stop."

"You didn't. You wouldn't..." He read the look in her eyes, panic in his face.

"I would and did," she said. All it took was an anonymous email to each paper. Every executive editor and every publisher had been listed as a recipient. The contents of the device were delivered to each. The time for deals, the time for negotiating, was over. "This ends now, Donald."

Stallworth jumped to his feet, stomping his heels against the floor. His fists squeezed nothing but air in front of him in powerless anger. "What have you done? Do you have any idea?"

"Discredited you? Damned you?" she said with an air of satisfaction. "After what you've taken from me, you deserve that and more."

"What I took?" Stallworth scoffed. "I have no idea—"

"No," she snapped. "That's not what this is about. Not the lies or the blame. People are dead. My people are dead. You've turned the entire law enforcement community against those that are left, and you're going to put a stop to it."

"I can't—"

"You can and you will," she said. The force of her words caused the burly man to shrink back to the edge of his chair. "You don't have a choice, Donald. Not with the shitstorm about to rain down on you. But I can mitigate the damage. I can give you an out. All you have to do is listen and do exactly what I tell you."

# CHAPTER TWENTY-FIVE

They ran for the elevator. The lower deck was empty, a surprise for sure to Zac, who waited to be caught as soon as they left the confines of the cell. April was more confident, unconcerned about interference. He wished for just a small piece of that unwavering faith that things would work out. But then, she hadn't lived through his last day.

April, the key to humanity's future, pulled him along. She didn't hesitate, didn't get sucked into the downward spiral of self-loathing that had become Zac's home. Every time he took a breath, every blink of his eyes brought back the memory of the dead—Lincoln, Metcalf, the scientists of the Cove. So many dead. He had betrayed everything he'd ever believed in at the DSA.

Was he doing the same thing to Sullivan?

No matter what he thought, no matter his former beliefs about secrets, lies and the DSA, the choice had been made the moment he entered the cell. April had initiated a countdown of some kind, the computers taken over by her directive. Zac still had yet to figure out her endgame, beyond escaping her current prison.

Around them, chaos ensued. The loss of the bright lights to the emergency reds, and the klaxon call of alarms ringing from every computer terminal, sent the population of the Cove rushing for the exit. Two more bodies would be lost in the mix, but the lone elevator made things more difficult.

April reached the end of the corridor first and jammed her thumb against the call button. The elevator was already on its way back up to the security station at the peak. Dozens waited their turn on the upper levels.

"We can't escape this way," she said.

Zac looked around for a secondary egress, some sign of an emergency exit. "Then how do we get out of here?" The countdown ticked away. Ten minutes remained. "And what exactly did you do?"

"Something you don't want to see for yourself," April replied. She grabbed his sleeve and yanked him toward the stairs. "Trust me, Zac."

"So where are we—"

"This way," she said. "Hurry."

They made it to the landing of the next level when the gunshot went off. Both stopped at the sound, which cut through the alarms and stomping feet echoing throughout the Cove.

"Not another step." Sullivan leveled his weapon on them; his brisk steps carried him from the far side of the deck.

"Sir," Zac called, his voice sheepish and soft. He quietly cursed himself for that weakness. Stepping in front of April, he shielded her from the man's anger. "Listen to me—"

"What have you done, Zac?" Sullivan snapped. "What have you been conspiring about with this one?"

"I haven't... I..." Zac tried to find the words, unsuccessful in the attempt. Sullivan's displeasure frightened him. Not only the gun, because he knew what the man could do with it, but the fire in his eyes. Sullivan was no longer the mild-mannered bureaucrat trying to improve the DSA's function, but a crazed maniac. His hair was ruffled, his collar twisted beneath his sweater. Even his neatly trimmed beard appeared shaggy and unkempt. The man's eyes were wide, like they would burst from his skull with the rage held within. "Sir, I—"

April pushed past Zac, unafraid. "It's over, Gregory. I've started a failsafe protocol in your precious Cove. Implosion is imminent."

*Implosion?* How had Zac not known? How had he ever been so stupid as to allow the Wellspring access to his computer? When the countdown began, he thought it might have been a lockdown to keep the contents of the Cove safe. She never suggested anything differently, never said a word about the catastrophe to come.

Sullivan had trusted him, had brought him on board to help

the world. Using the Wellspring's knowledge, they could affect actual change to people who needed it the most. That was what sold him on the mission. Then the death's started and Zac made a new choice. He chose a woman he knew nothing about, a stranger instead of his superior. Yet through it all, staring down the barrel of Sullivan's gun, Zac continued to stand by April.

Sullivan no longer even noticed his presence. Only April mattered to him, while the countdown bleated on from all sides. "You wouldn't dare."

April's lips curled. "There won't be anything left when it's over. The entire bluff will be wiped from the Earth like a bad memory."

The gun shook in Sullivan's hand. "Stop it. Turn it off. Now."

"Can't. Won't," April said with a shrug. "Doesn't matter which."

"Zac," Sullivan said, suddenly remembering the tech's presence. "Whatever she's told you is a lie. Help me stop this. The secrets here could save the world. No more war, no more hunger. All wiped out by us."

Zac wanted to believe him. He had wanted nothing more the moment the man had brought him into his plan. He thought he would be part of something bigger, like he'd always dreamed. His entire life, Zac had let others make the decisions for him.

He finally realized that to be the truth of the matter. Sullivan had been another in a long line of bad choices. It was time to do better — to *be* better.

"Us?" Zac shook his head. "You mean by you."

"Zac —"

"The ego on you," the tech continued. He cut Sullivan off from April. "That's all it's been about. Betraying my friends, watching Lincoln die? All so you could play God with power you don't understand. Power none of us has done a damn thing to deserve."

His entire body trembled, but he refused to stop, refused to back down. Zac took one step forward, then two, prompting Sullivan to backtrack along the deck.

"You're just like me," Zac said. "A sad shell of a man who never made the right choice for the right reasons. I won't help you."

Sullivan raised the gun to Zac's chest. "Then I have no use for you."

"No!"

Zac jumped at him and knocked the gun up. The shot boomed. The bullet shattered a monitor on the next level. Both men struggled for control of the weapon, teeth grinding and curses flying as they fought.

"Run, April!" Zac cried as he struggled for the gun.

"I'm not leaving you, Zac," April said, stuck in place. "There's no time."

"She's right," Sullivan said. "Let it go, Zac. I can forgive your confusion. Let it go, and we can make this right. I promise."

"To hell with your promises!"

Zac twisted hard on the man's wrist. In the act, Sullivan's finger slammed against the trigger, and a shot rang out. The gun fell between them. Sullivan scrambled for it, but Zac kicked it away.

"Zac…"

"I said run, April!"

"Zac…" April said again, her voice barely a whisper.

Zac turned. Blood ran in a thin stream from her chest. Her hands tried to cover the wound, but it did nothing to stem the tide. Her knees gave out, and she crumbled to the deck.

"No," Zac breathed, forgetting Sullivan—forgetting every-thing—to rush to her side. He pulled April close, and pressed on the wound to no avail.

Sullivan retrieved the gun. He loomed over them, aghast at the bleeding woman at his feet. "This can't be happening."

The countdown beeped all around them. Another minute was gone. Fear took over for Sullivan, and he bolted for the stairs.

"Sullivan!" Zac shouted. "Wait!"

The man was out of sight, on his way up the steps. Zac's vi-sion blurred, his eyes full of tears.

"I did this," he whispered. "This is all my fault."

# CHAPTER TWENTY-SIX

All around them, the complex quaked. The decking split from the walls, the terminals crashed loose from their anchors. Staffers and soldiers fled for the exit. The elevator was the only way out. The crews packed in tight before the car ascended, leaving dozens more stuck below.

During the interval, they raced for a higher level, hoping to make the next trip. Orders were shouted. The demands of superiors were ignored by those simply wanting to survive the impending countdown, which continued to blink on every terminal still connected to the system.

There were only eight minutes left. Until what, none of them knew. The only one who did was the woman who had initiated the strike. The woman who now lay cradled in Zac's arms as they watched the chaos and panic unfold around them.

Tears streamed down Zac's cheeks. He caught the wheezing of April's breath, the quick release of each one before the next as she fought to stay with him.

"Why?" Zac muttered. He wanted to scream. Finally, he had stood up and faced his fate like a man. Yet the result had been the same as if he had done nothing. The stream of blood from April's chest ran down his fingers as he applied pressure to the wound. There was too much blood. "Why did this have to happen?"

"That's not the right question, Zac," April said, her voice quiet against the pandemonium filling the Cove.

"I don't..." He took a breath and rubbed his eye along his shoulder to clear his vision. "April, I don't understand any of this."

Her hand reached up to graze his cheek. "You will."

"You were supposed to run," he said, frustration and anger mixed with exhaustion and sadness. "You could have gotten away. You… you're more important to this world than me."

"This isn't your fault, Zac. This was my choice to make." She shook her head. Her hand continued to rub lightly along his scruffy cheeks. "It's up to you now to see this through. It's your choice that sets the future, Zachary Modine."

"What do you mean?" he asked. He couldn't see two seconds into the future as it was. In the span of a day, he had burned every bridge he'd ever built. He had lost his wife and son over his desire for another woman. He had even failed to stand by Morgan in order to stay in Sullivan's good graces.

Self-preservation won out, and it cost him everything — including the woman in his arms. The Wellspring was a guide for the future, the means by which humanity reached the peak of its potential. Without her, without that guidance, what happened next? "April, I'm nobody. I can't change anything. I can't even save you."

"But you can," she whispered, her breathing faster now. Her time was running out while he whined about his misfortune. He was a selfish fool, always focused on the wrong thing, always worried about the public perception or about making the incorrect choice, when really there was only the choice and the consequence that followed.

April's hand tightened against his cheek. Her other reached up and grabbed the other cheek, pulling him closer. He let go of her wound; blood flowed freely from her chest.

"You choose the future, Zac. Remember that," she said. Tears filled her dim eyes. "And remember how sorry I am that it falls to you."

Her breathing stopped, and her chest refused to rise again. Her eyes faded to white. From the surface of her hands, light grew.

"What?" Light shone from her skin, then spread across her entire body. It jumped to Zac, enveloping him in the same glow. He couldn't see. He couldn't breathe. Zac tried to pry April's hands from his cheeks, tried to get free of the radiance filling his entire view. Her nails dug in tighter somehow, piercing his flesh in their need to remain.

The light engulfed them. The world disappeared. Only one sound remained; Zac heard his scream echoing throughout eternity.

# CHAPTER TWENTY-SEVEN

Morgan refused to take Kanigher's hand. She remained on her knees before him, a tight grip on a dead man's gun. Everything was moving too quickly around her. The lights were still out, the emergency reds blanketing the immense complex in crimson. She could hear the frantic steps of personnel heading for the lone elevator exit, while others clattered up and down the stairwells on either end of the deck. They fled, and she stayed put, unsure how to act or who to trust.

"How long?" she asked the man standing in front of her. She had never heard the name Kanigher before today, had never seen his face during her tenure at the DSA. Yet he claimed loyalty to Metcalf, a spy within the NSA's ranks.

"Excuse me?"

Her grip tightened on the Glock. "How long has Metcalf had you on the inside?"

"Since the beginning," Kanigher replied. His gaze flitted around the decking. His concern was on their position, open and unprotected, while hers was on surviving the next minute with a man she didn't know the first thing about. "Susan is crafty like that."

"That's one word for it," Morgan snapped. "Manipulative is another."

Kanigher pulled his hand back. "And another is protective. Of her team and her mission."

Morgan stood on her own. She kept the gun at her side. "To the point of compromising both. Or maybe I am by going along with you."

"Are we really going to do this now?" Kanigher pointed to

the gun in disbelief.

"I don't know you."

"Get over it," he said. "After what I just did?"

Martin lay dead beside them. He would have killed Morgan without a second thought. She might have done the same had their roles been reversed; her ethical judgment over such matters bordered on non-existent after being awake for almost two days straight. The deed, however, clearly weighed heavily on Kanigher, who could barely look at the body.

"I served with Martin for six years," Kanigher continued. "I went to his daughter's baptism. I stood at his wedding. You know what they're going to go through, thanks to me? I have to live with that now. All to save your stubborn ass."

Pain sat in his swollen eyes. He tried to display a hard edge, but she saw straight through to the heart of the man. Pulling the trigger was a last resort to him. If he hadn't gone for a kill shot, she would have been dead, the mission forever compromised. He was the man on the inside, and he was willing to work with her, having never done so in the past. How could she do any less, given the circumstances?

She tucked the gun away, then extended her hand. "You're right."

He took the offer with a sad smile. "Good. Now let's get moving."

"Any idea what happened to the lights?" Morgan asked as they started down the deck for the stairs. Kanigher paused at the computer terminal at the end of the corridor.

"That's not my primary concern at the moment," he said. He moved aside to offer her a better view. The computer had not gone completely blank in the power outage. In the corner was a small counter, ticking closer and closer to zero. "Come on. We might be able to stop the countdown if we locate the source."

He led her lower, to the depths of the complex. It made sense considering the secrecy involved and the importance of their target, but with each level behind them, Morgan worried she would never see the light of day again. That there would only be darkness ahead in all they did.

Morgan stopped at the base of the stairs. A flash of white beamed from the far side of the deck plating. "Hold up," she called. "I thought I saw..."

Two figures lay on the ground. They were only silhouettes at first, but slowly sharpened into focus as she recognized one of them.

"Zac?"

The shining light disappeared, and the emergency reds took over once again. Kanigher tried to pull her back, but it was too late. Morgan raced across the deck, her boots clattering loudly against the metal. Zac was curled over another figure, an old woman from the looks of it.

"Zac!" Morgan fell to her knees at his side. The woman in his arms dropped to the grating, her body pale and lifeless. For a moment, Morgan feared the same of Zac. Morgan had connected with him, loved him, to no small degree. When Grissom had shown up, Morgan believed she'd never lay eyes on the charming tech again. She wanted the chance to talk about their night together, to make her case for why their relationship worked so well. The very thought of losing him brought tears to her eyes. "Zac, please. Don't be —"

Zac stirred. His head lolled upon her shoulder. "What? Who?"

"Thank God," Morgan whispered. Her hand grazed his cheek until his eyes snapped wide.

"Morgan?" he said in surprise. "Where did you come from?"

She didn't bother to reply. Part of her couldn't find the words, while the rest worried about ruining the moment with another fight, another argument. She hadn't come for him, anyway.

Helping Zac to his feet, she returned to the fallen woman at his side. She appeared to be in her mid-seventies with wavy silver-white hair. Morgan searched for a pulse, then noticed the gunshot wound to her chest.

"Is this her?"

Kanigher offered a frustrated nod, hands to his hips. "Yeah."

"She saved me," Zac said. He was lost at the sight of the woman. What had they gone through together? There was something in the way he looked at her, some connection Morgan couldn't possibly fathom.

"Zac, I —"

"Hate to break it up, folks," Kanigher interrupted. He shifted to a nearby terminal. He typed in a code for access without success. The timer continued to tick away. Only four minutes remained. "I don't know how to get this thing to stop. It's tied to the internal systems somehow. I don't think we can bypass it."

"You can't," Zac confirmed, still gazing down at the woman so sought after. "She wanted it that way."

"Great," Kanigher said. "Any suggestions?"

"I have one," Morgan said. She pulled Zac away from the dead and toward the stairs. "But we need to move."

Kanigher groaned. "I need a new job."

"I'll help you with your résumé if we get the hell out of here in time," Morgan said, taking the lead.

They started their climb to the lab with the ventilation shaft. The countdown continued to tick away.

"I am not liking our chances," Kanigher muttered under his breath.

"Neither am I," Morgan said with a huff, turning the corner for the next flight of stairs. "Neither am I."

# CHAPTER TWENTY-EIGHT

Stallworth paced the length of the living room. His hand shook, spilling drops of his bourbon to the floor. His ruminations went on for minutes. The back-and-forth pacing, combined with the constant refilling of his drink, was tedious to watch from Metcalf's chair in the corner.

She checked the clock on the wall, the time slowly ticking away. The morning shows were in full swing, the news provided by Metcalf no doubt plastered on every front page in the country and leading most of the chatter. The noose tightened around Stallworth's neck—hence the drinking, the sweating, and the cursing under his breath.

"Finished?" she asked after his latest lap.

He failed to reply, the grumbling inaudible under his breath. Instead, he returned to the bar and filled the glass again. He took a heavy gulp, too much at once, and the liquor ran down his chin in a thin stream.

"Dammit," he muttered. He patted at the stain along his wrinkled shirt, then surrendered. Placing the glass on the counter, he leaned against the wood. Deep breaths centered him as he turned his back to her. "You've damned me, Susan. You sit there and smile while you condemn me to death. The Trust—"

"Is your own doing," she snapped. "That was your choice. Now, I'll say it one more time. Are you finished?"

His head fell to his chest. Fingers stretched across the bar, then squeezed against the wood. His body trembled with anger—impotent against the allegations leaked to the media. There was no play here, no choice to be made. There was only an end to things. Anything else was denial and arrogance, of which the blustery man held in abundance.

The glass returned to his hand, and he finished the bourbon inside. He wiped his chin with his sleeve and set the glass aside before turning to face her once more. His heavy steps carried him back to the chair, where he collapsed against the cushion. His hand fell to his brow.

"Say your piece already."

Metcalf sighed at his petulance. He played the victim of circumstance, when he had been handed everything in his life: power, prestige, and the means to accomplish anything as long as it met the approval of his betters. Unfortunately for him, he revolted at the wrong time, and now he paid the price for his actions whether he liked it or not.

"I want a full confession," she said. He nearly jumped back to his feet, but she pressed on—ready for his reaction. "On camera, not some backroom deal. You will stand trial for the formation of the DSA and the explosion that ended it. You will resign from your position and face justice."

"Absurd. You must be out of your damn mind, Susan, if you think that will ever happen."

"It will, Donald," Metcalf replied, leaning close. "You're *going* to do this."

"I'll never live that long."

Metcalf laughed. Her eyes washed over his massive frame. "Not with your diet, no."

Stallworth's cheeks reddened. "The Trust will—"

"Have greater concerns than a fallen ally," she answered. She understood the stakes and what was required to keep Stallworth onboard as a willing participant in what came next. "There will be no jail time for you—no great reprisal. Just a quiet disgrace with the usual sweeping under the rug to keep the American people content."

His eyes softened at her assertion. "You... you would do that for me? After all, I... all Sullivan brought against you?"

"No," Metcalf said. She stood and rounded the table. "You don't get to pass the buck on any of this. Sullivan might have brought you into this, but you made your own bed. People are dead because of you. I... I lost too much because of you."

"Grissom," Stallworth said. "I know, Susan, and if there was any—"

The back of her hand connected soundly with his cheek. "How long? Did you make him a deal? Did you blackmail him as easily as I did you?"

"Nothing of the sort," Stallworth said, rubbing at the wound.

Another slap, this time to the other cheek. "Liar! Jake would never have worked for you."

"He didn't work for me!" Stallworth admitted. "Grissom worked for the Trust. He always worked for the Trust, ever since his time in the military."

*Always?* He had lied to her right from the start? Metcalf took a step back. Her chest heaved to calm herself. Grissom had been her second-in-command and the man she'd trusted with practically every secret she ever held. All the while, he had played her.

"Listen," Stallworth pleaded. "I never would have done any of that. Not to you. Not to Grissom. Greg pushed for Asset Control after the Oliver Blake fiasco. He reconditioned him into that abomination that killed those people. Those two cops. And... and that secretary of yours."

"Stephanie Atwater," Metcalf said, teeth clenched. "Her name was Stephanie Atwater."

"Exactly. Greg was the one behind it all. Not me. Never me."

"He'll get his. I promise you that. But you? You're going to fix this mess before resigning. You're going to make this right, Donald."

He read her cold stare clearly. Every member of the field team had been accused of treason, thanks to Sullivan. Law enforcement had hunted them and that would never stop unless they were cleared of the charges.

"I can't," Stallworth said. "I can't just wave my hand and take it all back. You're terrorists in the eyes of the law."

"Wrong." She crouched beside his chair. Her hand reached out and snatched his tie, pulling him close. "We're the ghosts in the system, and you're going to make sure we stay that way from you and your friends in the Trust. And all those people who lost their livelihoods, the hundreds employed by the DSA, are going to find jobs in other departments without reprisal, Donald. You're going to put that in place at once."

"If I don't? If I fight you?"

She pushed him and he slammed against the chair. Standing, she brushed her hands clean along the length of her coat. "You'll lose. You have ten hours to get it done, Donald. I'll be watching."

Metcalf didn't wait for a reply, and Stallworth gave none. Her confident stride carried her toward the front door. She was unafraid of the guards outside. Stallworth was a broken man without a defense.

Still, she felt the need to look back when she reached the edge of the living room. Stallworth's bloodshot gaze tracked her. Sweat continued to gleam off his forehead.

"I'd change your shirt and maybe shave," Metcalf said with a smirk. "You'll want to look your best for the cameras."

"Where are you going?" he called after her. "What are you going to do next?"

"That's not your concern any longer." She opened the front door. The light of the morning sun filled the corridor. She waved to the broken man left behind. "Enjoy your retirement, Donald."

# CHAPTER TWENTY-NINE

Adler leaned against a tree overlooking the bluff where the massive complex was hidden from view. She read her scanner to see the heat signatures racing back and forth across the screen. They appeared as little dots, but their frantic pace—the way they dropped in and out of view—caused her to imagine them as small Pac-Man's running for their lives from the ghosts in the machine.

There was nothing she could do. Ever since Morgan entered the ventilation shaft to infiltrate the rogue operation, static had filled their communication line. Adler expected as much with the background radiation pouring from the structure. Nothing dangerous from what she estimated, but it failed to appease her. The readings emanated from every level of the complex, not a singular source. It was everywhere and blanketed all communication between her and Morgan.

Nonetheless, Adler made another attempt to break through the static. "Morgan? Morgan, do you read me?"

She had asked the question every two minutes since she'd lost sight of the woman. Her watch kept track of the next interval, ticking away the seconds of crackling pops in her ear.

Disappointment was something she had grown accustomed to in life. The first occurrence happened when she had been six years old: her father had forgotten to pick her up at school. He wasn't the most attentive to detail, always more fixated on the local bar scene than anything related to his daughter. The realization that he didn't truly care if she lived or died had been a wake-up call. She'd witnessed the same blasé behavior in most people around her—from teachers to childhood friends. She had held them to a higher standard, yet always met with the same disappointment.

It had clouded every relationship. Her desire to deliver—to carry the burden of elevating those around her—had made for a lonely existence. She, however, used those skills to the best of her ability to look at the bigger picture. Their weakness, those of drugs or booze or even simple avarice, were endemic in society itself and could not be blamed on the individual. So it was society that had to change.

Adler had scored top marks in college, majoring in political science and sociology. Government work fascinated her. Her propensity at logistics learned from a lifetime of scheduling her own rides to and from school, as well as figuring out her next meal when the house remained empty at all hours of the day and night, had made her the perfect candidate.

Metcalf had agreed, and recruited her to the DSA. Adler's ability to blend in made her the perfect undercover agent: off the books and independent of the primary operation. Adler had jumped at the chance, helping to bring about the change she'd hoped to instill in everyone around her for so long.

Now she was the disappointment. Morgan required backup, someone to actually be in the compound with her, or at the very least, provide useful intel from the sideline. Adler did neither. She offered nothing in the way of assistance.

Her abilities had only carried her so far. Now that the DSA had been forced underground because of Sullivan's work, Adler found herself in a downward spiral of self-pity. She had hoped Morgan would pull her out of it, that by helping her infiltrate the compound, it would reignite her drive.

It had accomplished the opposite, and Adler could do nothing but wait for Morgan's return—if she ever did.

"Come on, Morgan," she muttered with a hand to her ear. The static raged louder. "Just give me a sign. Let me know I didn't send you in there to die."

Her answer came in a rumble beneath her feet. The ground shook, and a mild tremor spread across the bluff where she stood. Across the way, however, the tremor was more extreme.

"What the hell?"

She held tight to the tree to maintain her balance. The red dots faded from view on her screen. Looking across the way, she saw the small monitor station at the peak of the bluff. Personnel flowed from its doors; they ran for the parking lot at the end of the entry road.

Military personnel and civilians alike fled; their steps were awkward due to the shaking ground at their feet. The world rumbled louder and louder, only drowned out by the screeching of transports racing away from the scene.

The explosion came quick, and the ground hiding the complex ruptured in all directions. With it came a shockwave that lasted mere seconds. The ground that had sprung up in the blast was suddenly pulled back in reverse. The entire bluff caved in on itself in a massive implosion.

Everything was sucked in its direction. Pulled forcibly from her position by the event, Adler fell to her knees. She hugged the ground, eyes locked on the bluff that continued to collapse inward.

Her scanner pinged in her grasp. The sound was incessant, loud, and demanded attention. A mass of electromagnetic energy screamed across her screen. All came from the collapsed structure and spread in every direction once it escaped. To Adler, it appeared to be a radio wave unlike any she had ever seen before.

"A signal," she whispered as she made her way to her feet. Her scanners tried to decipher the meaning, tried to pull its trajectory or ultimate destination, to no avail. All her equipment, everything that had read the surge so clearly, faded to black. "How? Where the hell did it go?"

The bluff across the way had turned into a pile of rubble and debris. Grass had overturned, sucked into the implosion, leaving only dirt and stone in its way. Screams filled the air, unseen and terrified. A few stragglers continued to flee from the small monitor station that teetered over in the aftershock of the event.

"Morgan?" Adler called into the comm. There was no more static. Silence filled the channel. "Please, Morgan. Tell me you made it out. Please."

# CHAPTER THIRTY

The explosion hit while they were in the ventilation shaft. Kanigher was in the lead, crawling along the metal. Beyond him was the light, almost blinding compared to the darkness at their rear.

It reminded Zac of another light, one seen when April had passed in his arms. It had stolen the world away from him. Somehow he had lost four whole minutes to the blinding light in the aftermath of April's death, yet he could not address the lost time. What had happened to him? Why did he sense a tingling behind his eyes and a nervous energy rushing through his entire body?

He chalked up the strange sensation to their escape. Soldiers and fleeing support staff had locked the elevator down. They had no time to wait for another car. Morgan knew of only one other way, her point of entry to the facility. How she had found the Cove in the first place was asked but never answered. Nothing he said garnered a response as they ran to the lab where the shaft was located.

Morgan shuffled through the tunnel before him. Her hands were balled up into fists, her focus clearly on the ticking clock behind them. Not on finding Zac inside the Cove, or the dead woman they had been forced to leave behind.

They had almost made it when the world shook.

"Move! Move!" Kanigher shouted, but there was no way to reach the torn grate. The explosion hit with such force that the shaft teetered. It wrenched forward and the world outside shifted. Kanigher reached for the grate, then turned back to the others. "Stop!"

Dirt and debris fell from the cliff side, and the shaft became dislodged from the main core of the complex. The vent shook and bent, the weight of the three of them at one end too much. The shaft pitched forward in the blast. Instead of a view of the bluff ahead, there was only the water below.

"Back it up, Zac!" Kanigher yelled as they fell.

The impact against the water felt like a punch to the gut. Zac's hands pushed him backward for the now open end of the pipe in a struggle for freedom. Water rushed inside, filling the space in an instant. Zac took a deep breath. The pipe fell away as he reached open water. Morgan followed quickly, though she held her position at the end of the shaft to offer Kanigher a hand out. All three breached the surface, then fought for the rocky shore.

The bluff collapsed above them. The force of their expulsion had been nothing compared to the aftermath. Earth rained down like hellfire over them, massive clumps from the surface propelled outward by the force of the blast. Just as quickly, the rain ended and the entire side of the cliff collapsed into the water. Everything else was pulled toward the Cove, sucked inside and crushed. April had set the complex to cave in on itself; the resulting implosion had buried all trace of the wonders hidden inside the cliff.

Kanigher reached the shore near the adjacent bluff first. The move put some distance from the Cove where debris continued to shower down from above. Trees dislodged from the still shifting surface, while brush and foliage crashed around them in the water.

Zac pulled himself up on the rocks. His body ached from the effort, and he struggled to free himself from the water completely. He reached for a hand up, but was ignored as Kanigher moved to assist Morgan.

"Here, Morgan," Kanigher called. He lifted her to the shore, and the pair made it clear of the rushing waves for the small inlet. Morgan coughed loudly, water sputtering from her lips. "Try to take it easy."

She shook her head and waved him back. One final cough flew free, and the last of the water splashed to the rocks beneath her. Then Morgan stood tall, hands on her hips. She always had to be that way, independent and strong in the face of others.

"I'm fine," she said. She turned to face the cliff side. Frustration filled the deep browns of her eyes. "If I had been a few minutes earlier, been faster in getting here, she would still be alive."

"You don't know that," Kanigher replied.

Zac sat, his feet still in the water. That was the reason for Morgan's surprise at seeing him. She hadn't arrived at the Cove for him, hadn't infiltrated the enemy stronghold in some chivalrous exercise to save his hide from a terrible decision. No, she had come for the Wellspring. She chased the same prize as everyone else. No one had come for Zac.

"Do you?" Morgan shot back to Kanigher. "You were on the inside. Do you know what this was all about? Any of it?"

Kanigher shook his head. "Only what Sullivan and Stallworth shared. So not much, unfortunately."

"Figures."

Zac tried to stand and slipped. His hands slammed on the jagged edges of a rock. His ankle twisted from the fall. Lifting from the shore, his palms cut and covered with fresh blood — his own this time — Zac reached out for the pair.

"Morgan? Can I get a hand? Do you mind — ?"

Morgan didn't budge from her spot. Her arms crossed her chest as she loomed over him in judgment. "She's dead, Zac. The Wellspring is dead."

Zac shuffled for the shore. He winced at the pain shooting from his hands. Rubbing them along his soaked clothing seemed to help for the moment. His ankle, though, swelled.

"I was there, Morgan," he said. "It was Sullivan." He raised his hand once more. "Please, can you give me some help here?"

Morgan shook her head and backed up a step. "You had nothing to do with what happened?"

"I didn't! Sullivan shot her. I tried to stop him."

"Did you?" she asked in disbelief. "You were working with him! You chose him over Metcalf — over me! He used you to get to us, tracking us through your system. Stephanie Atwater is dead because you helped that man. Ben too, as far as I know."

More were dead because of his choice. More were dead because he didn't have the strength to stand up, because he had failed to see the consequences of his actions.

"I didn't know, all right?" he said. "Yes, I was upset with

Metcalf and I fed intel to Sullivan, but how could I possibly know how he would use it? I didn't mean for this to happen, Morgan. Not the Wellspring. Not Lincoln or—"

"Lincoln?" Morgan asked. The name caused her lips to quiver and her eyes to turn from righteous fury to sadness. She nearly collapsed at the sound of his name. "You're saying he's..."

She didn't finish the thought, couldn't finish it. Neither could he. The anger returned and Morgan turned away from Zac. Slow steps carried her toward Kanigher and the path out of the rocky shoals for the peak of the bluff.

Zac dragged himself up, his ankle screaming in pain. He didn't care. None of it mattered to him as he shuffled ahead. "Morgan! Wait!"

He grabbed at her wrist and she wheeled around. Her hand was at his throat. She squeezed, forcing him against the cliff side.

"Morgan, don't!" Kanigher said, but made no move against her.

Zac could see it in her eyes—the love they once held, and how he had dashed it away.

"You let Lincoln die too?" Pain infiltrated every word. Her eyes stung him with their sadness, not at the loss of the man, but at the betrayal of someone she had grown so close to recently. He deserved every accusation, every recrimination. He earned her hate. "Who the hell are you? How could I have ever felt... ever been with someone like you?"

She let go of his throat and stepped back. Zac rubbed at the soreness, spreading little drops of blood from his palm. With his other hand, Zac held onto the cold earth for support. "I screwed up, Morgan. But I can make things right. You have to let me try to fix this. Please."

"No. I don't."

"Morgan!"

Her steps carried her past Kanigher for the trail to the peak. He hesitated at her side, his own judgment clear in his stony stare. Then he followed her.

"It was a mistake, Morgan, but I can help! I want to help!" Zac left the wall to chase them. His ankle refused to support his weight, and he tumbled to the ground. Sand and muck covered his face, but through it all, he saw the woman he'd loved so fiercely peer back at him in disgust.

"Help yourself, Zac," she said. "No one else will now."

With that, they departed without a single glance back. He had lost them, lost his second chance, because of his choices. Thirty-two hours was all it had taken to ruin his entire life.

Zac was on his own now.

# CHAPTER THIRTY-ONE

The elevator shook beneath Sullivan's feet. Cables rattled as the tremor took hold of the entire hill. The car pinged and the doors slowly opened when the explosion let loose from underground.

Sullivan leaped for the safety of the monitor station. His shoulder slammed into the opening door. The collision shunted him hard to the right, and he crashed to the ground with a cry of pain. He grabbed at his arm, applying pressure on the point of impact. No doubt there was damage beneath the surface. He was no longer a young man—every bump and bruise turned out to be a torn ligament or muscle sprain.

There wasn't time for further analysis. The explosion rumbled deep within the Cove's infrastructure. The elevator shook, his leg still within the door frame. Suddenly, the cable snapped. Sullivan pulled his leg back a second before the car descended.

Slow to move, Sullivan shuffled closer to the tube for a look. The car shattered upon impact at the base of the Cove. All that remained in its place was a gaping hole—a dismal pit leading straight to hell itself.

The shockwave silenced. In its place, the ground began to crack and split. Sullivan scrambled in a crawl from the elevator for the exit. The monitor station—the false-front presented to the public—was being pulled down. Whatever the Wellspring had started, her so-called final failsafe, it resulted in the complete destruction of anything within reach.

Fear threatened to swallow Sullivan as completely as the earth beneath him. The aging bureaucrat, with eyes panicked and hands begging for someone to reach out and rescue him, fought for the exit. His feet kicked the ground, which crumbled seconds after he shifted away from the growing implosion.

It wasn't until sunlight hit his face that he realized he had escaped the monitor station. Sullivan rolled along the sidewalk, farther and farther from the teetering structure. The roof snapped in two. Large beams filled the confines of the cramped room. Smoke and dust rose in a plume away from the devastation that filled the entire cavernous wonderland he had hoped to use for the benefit of the world.

The Cove was gone.

Sullivan, his body wound tight from the ordeal, slowly made it to his feet. His entire world had been stolen from him — every dream and advancement. His legacy had been stripped from him by the Wellspring's actions.

That wasn't the end of it for him, though. Sirens blared from down the road. His soldiers continued to flee in droves. Transports raced away from the calamity. All traces of the lab, of the breathtaking technology, had been lost in the implosion — buried under a mountain of rock and dirt. There would be no legacy, no great coup for him to spearhead. Only escape remained.

Where his soldiers met resistance to the south in the form of curious law enforcement agents, Sullivan limped with haste north for the remaining tree line. Staggered steps in dirt-laden shoes carried him along the pavement. His heart pounded in his chest for a break, but he could not slow down.

It wasn't until he entered the small patch of forest that he allowed a long breath of relief to escape. He had survived — that had to mean something. He would *make* it mean something. There had to be a way to continue without the Wellspring, without the resources of the DSA at his disposal.

He needed to call Stallworth, to rally behind what few allies remained, and come up with a new strategy. His legacy would endure this setback.

Sullivan left the tragedy of the Cove behind for the thickening foliage to the north. His pace slowed. The pressing need for escape was less of a concern now that he was out of sight, and he worried about the throbbing pain in his shoulder. Having it looked at became a priority, right alongside the list of calls to his allies for help.

All were forgotten in an instant. Three men waited for him in the center of the forest. Two of them carried weapons. The third never required such a direct sign of aggression. His words held much more bite than the sting of a bullet.

"I'm disappointed, Greg," the man in the pale suit said.

"Hollis," Sullivan said, the name bitter against his lips. David Hollis was the man behind the Trust, and the figurehead Sullivan had sought to dethrone through his actions. Hollis had given Sullivan his second chance and a purpose through their work at the Trust. It was all kept secret, the operations and the goals hidden from view, something Sullivan could never stomach.

"Of all people, I thought we shared the same vision," Hollis said, false sincerity in his eyes.

"Spare me your condemnation," Sullivan spat, defiant in the face of the armed contingent before him. "You would sit on technology undreamed of — advancements beyond our imagination!"

Hollis nodded. "For the good of all."

"To protect your interests."

"Humanity is my interest," Hollis replied. "Our continued existence is my interest. Yours was ego and notoriety. You've exposed our operations. You've set back plans decades in the making. What do you have to say for yourself, Greg?"

"Stallworth —"

Hollis' hand rose, a finger silencing him. "He will be dealt with. In time."

Desperation took hold. Sullivan pawed at his sweater vest to make himself presentable. "I know how this looks. I know I went outside the lines on this one. But give me another chance. You'll see."

"I gave you a second chance, Greg," Hollis said. "This was that chance."

"What do you mean?"

Hollis stepped over to the panicked man. His hand fell on Sullivan's wounded shoulder and squeezed. He leaned close when Sullivan flinched, Hollis' words barely a whisper over the sound of nature surrounding them.

"I knew about Buffalo, Greg," he said. "The truth behind the break-in at our Wex operation. I looked the other way, cleaned up your mess, hoping you'd see the error of your way."

"I... David, I —"

Hollis let go of his shoulder. "But you failed. Like always."

He turned his back to Sullivan. It was his final dismissal of the man and it was more than Sullivan could take. He had endured such behavior from his fellow man for decades, always casting him aside rather than embracing the vision he held for the world.

"Don't you dare," Sullivan snapped. "Don't you turn your back on me! Do you know who I am?"

Hollis stopped. Tilting his head back at Sullivan, his lips curled slightly. "I know exactly who you are."

Sullivan felt heat rise from his chest. He heard the snapping of the air around him as the two silent players in their discussion opened fire on him. All breath left his body and his knees gave way.

Hollis led his men away from the scene, not bothering to look back at the deed done, not bothering to wait for the end. It was the last thing Greg Sullivan saw before he collapsed along the soft earth—tossed aside in the refuse of history—alone and ultimately forgotten.

# CHAPTER THIRTY-TWO

A sparse crowd loitered in the dining area of the Empire Garden Restaurant. Two men argued in the corner over which dish was healthier for them. The answer was neither, but that hadn't stopped them from ordering the pork egg rolls instead of the vegetable variety. A young woman sat at the entrance, enthralled by the local entertainment leaflet with its selection of concerts. She circled every third option on what would most likely be a busy week.

Metcalf stood in a cramped area near the counter. Steam rose from various spots on the other side; the crackling of the fryer sent little pops in her ear. She tried to ignore the surrounding distractions without drawing attention to herself. She wore a pair of sunglasses, despite the fading sun in the distance, and a plain black ball cap. While she waited for her meal, she focused on the television hanging in the corner.

The press conference was in full swing. She couldn't help but smirk at the man behind the podium. Stallworth had followed her advice to the best of his ability. He wore his best suit—navy blue—with a silk red tie over his white button-down. His cheeks were flushed and the lights from the news crews only accentuated the sweat glommed on his skin.

"—that I am resigning effective immediately," Stallworth said as Metcalf focused on the sound once more instead of the armed men surrounding the stage. Stallworth let the words settle over the crowd. He sipped at a small cup of water before returning to what must have been hastily crafted notes in the aftermath of their meeting. "Under my direction, a shadow organization known as the Department of Special Assignments was created and hidden from elected officials. While I never sought to commit any wrongdoings through this unsupervised and unlawful group, others under my leadership went astray, leading to the calamity witnessed in downtown Bethesda yesterday."

In the corner of the screen, the news cut to an image of the DSA warehouse crumbling in a cloud of dust. The image, captured by amateur video, was taken from blocks away yet remained a clear view of the building's destruction. Metcalf's hand reached for the counter and her eyes closed for a moment at the sight of the loss of what had become her home for the last decade.

"This was no terrorist act," Stallworth said, the words blunt and slow in their utterance. The message was not for the viewer, but for her. It accompanied the text sent to her just before the broadcast. The names of every agent under her command, from researcher to field team, had been scrubbed from his server. There would be no more threat against the innocents caught in the middle of Sullivan's power grab. They were safe again from reprisal. Metcalf had given him a deadline, and he'd met it with mere minutes to spare. *The typical bureaucrat.*

Stallworth cleared his throat and dabbed at his brow. "This was merely a mistake, a setback, in my pledge to protect the country I love. I was wrong to do so without authorization and will face any punishment deemed appropriate by my superiors and the American people. Thank you."

The crowd erupted with questions—none of which were answered. Agents flanking Stallworth pulled him away from the podium for the waiting car. The media deserved the whole truth. Unfortunately, it was time to offer answers to his superiors, who no doubt called in every favor to squelch any further coverage of the event.

Metcalf smiled as Stallworth faded from view and the talking heads began their endless and useless debate over the man's confession. "Goodbye, Donald."

A short Asian woman plopped three large brown paper bags on the counter next to the register. She peered around the room, double checking the receipt through thick glasses. "Order for Susan?"

Metcalf nodded. "That's me."

She passed along the money without being asked, not caring

about the cost of the meal. Her attention remained on the television and the aftermath of Stallworth's confession. It was the only play she had left, to put the onus on him and take the spotlight away from the DSA and her personnel.

Change fell across her waiting palm, and she pocketed it quickly. The older woman stared her down, then pointed for the door. "You need help carrying?"

"I've got it," Metcalf replied. She took the bags in hand, careful to keep them locked beneath her fingertips.

"Big celebration?" the woman asked from behind the counter.

Metcalf glanced back at the screen. The news replayed footage of Stallworth's worried face as he left the conference. In the background, one of the agents surrounding him carried a pair of cuffs, which the broadcast had been nice enough to circle and enhance for the viewer.

Metcalf's smile widened. "More like a good start."

She headed for the door and the fading light of day, ready for the next challenge.

# CHAPTER THIRTY-THREE

Snow tripped up the traction of the sedan, and he veered back into the narrow strip of cleared pavement worn down by the light traffic over the last few hours. Ben drove in uncomfortable silence.

The snow flew toward the speeding vehicle like flecks of light against the darkness. The windshield wipers did little to clear them away and obscured his vision more than they came to his aid. Farm country surrounded him on both sides. Sprawling fields and small homes dotted the roadside. All were dark in the late hour; the clouds offered no hint of the moon hidden behind them.

Ben clutched tightly to the note in his hand. He read the address again. The listing was in Odenton, some place he had never been, never even heard of until a few hours earlier. The address hadn't exactly come from a reliable source.


Ben stood in the thick silence of the motel room. There was more to say, but every thought turned to anger, and every question rang so loudly it blotted out any possibility for a rational conversation. After their heated discussion over his role to come, Ben realized none of it mattered if his colleagues failed to survive the day. His ploy with Sullivan had been with only that one goal in mind, yet he still knew nothing of his team's fate. The Witness clearly recognized the sullen silence offered by the man he had saved and held out the note.

"What's this?"

"You're worried about your friends," the Witness said. "This is where they will be."

"How could you possibly—?" Ben stopped himself from finishing the question. The Witness simply knew, and had always known, details which escaped everyone else. Ben looked closer at the note. The writing style wasn't that of the man before him, but was one he had come to recognize over the last few months. Susan Metcalf *was* alive; the note confirmed the truth spouted by the Witness.

When Ben glanced up, the Witness was holding a set of keys. He tossed them to the confused agent, who caught them.

"There's a car outside. I have no intention of keeping you from your colleagues a moment longer."

Ben's hand encircled the keys. "Right. You really think I'm just going to walk out that door? That I could let you go free after what you've done?"

"That's exactly what you're going to do," the Witness replied with a smirk.

"Yeah? We've done this song and dance before, is that it?"

The Witness shook his head. "Not at all. I merely know the man you believe yourself to be."

"And that is?"

"A good one," the Witness said, his words sincere. "A good friend."

Ben bit the inside of his cheek. He wrestled with his desire for answers against his uncertainty regarding his team—to his friends. Turning away from the Witness, Ben retrieved a pair of shoes by the door and the clothes hanging over the chair in the room's corner. He dressed without a word.

His friends needed him. Ben had sacrificed himself to keep them safe. Now that he was back on his feet, he could do no less. Prepared for the snowy weather with a coat in hand, Ben reached for the handle.

The Witness stopped him. "You're welcome, Agent Riley."

"Don't." Ben took a step toward his so-called savior, animosity rising to the surface. "This? Whatever you did to me? *For* me? It doesn't make us even. Not after what you did in Bellbrook. Not after what you did to Ruth. You're still going to pay."

"But not today."

Ben left without another word.

Reaching the address, Ben turned into the narrow driveway of the property. It was a yellow farmhouse, brought to life through the dim haze of the sedan's headlights. A white picket fence surrounded the house, and in the background were the branches of a wide orchard. He circled around the home, the snow crunching beneath his tires, until he came to a large hill. A metal door covered the front. Standing before the door was Metcalf.

She wore a heavy wool coat and hugged tight for warmth. A ball cap covered her auburn locks. Ben brought the car to a halt before her and silenced the engine. He hesitated to exit, unsure of what to say. She had been waiting for him to arrive, had known he was on his way. There was only one way for that to be possible in his mind.

The door opened, and he clambered out into the cold. The headlights shone for a brief instant, then faded to darkness when he shut the door.

"Ben," she called with excitement in her voice. The joy made her sound younger than usual—almost human—compared to the cold calculation that had accompanied most of their time together at the DSA. It pained him to hear. "It's good to see you up and about. I was—"

"Stop," Ben replied. "Just stop."

Metcalf took a step back, concerned at his response. "Ben—"

"I know what you did for me," he said, unable to look at her. He kept his eyes locked on the snow falling in the distance and the dead trees lining the back acres of the property. "I know you saved my life by turning to him. But this... where we go from here isn't going to go the way it did before."

"I'm not sure what you mean," she said. Her hand reached for his shoulder.

"You know him, Metcalf," Ben said, the words quiet against the wind. "You know him well enough to ask him for help. That means you've known him a helluva lot longer than you've ever mentioned."

"Ben." Her hand fell away from him and back into her pocket. The excitement was gone. The joy at seeing him faded. "Don't ask me. Please."

"I won't," he said. "Not today. You saved my life. You deserve the reprieve."

"Thank—"

"Don't you dare thank me." His eyes locked with hers. "I might not be asking the question, but someone will. You damn well better have an answer ready when it happens. For all our sakes."

She nodded, silence following them as they made their way to the hill. Ben stepped inside the silo and watched the doors close before him. He came to help his colleagues, to save what he could after being saved himself.

He only hoped it was the right decision.

# CHAPTER THIRTY-FOUR

Metcalf waited outside in the hall. She opened the door and allowed Ben first entry into the Bunker. He stood just inside the wide entryway, like he had stepped into another world.

Overhead lights ran in rows along the ten-foot high ceiling. To the right were storage lockers and a supply closet. The door was ajar, and Ben noted several tools and weapons locked inside. To the left was an opulent kitchen. Cabinetry lined the wall, a stove and grill opposite the sink. There was counter space with stools, as well as three tables with chairs for eating.

A staging area had been set up in the center of the room, before a metal staircase descended into what appeared to be an intricate monitor womb. Computer terminals were positioned below the large television screens. Every screen sat blank at the moment.

Sitting at the table of what could only be the operations area were the remnants of the Department of Special Assignments. At the time of Ben's recruitment, over two hundred people had been employed at the agency. Three remained.

They picked at their plates, bags of takeout spread among them. The sound of laughter and camaraderie flowed up to his position as he moved in for a closer look.

"Are you hoarding the lo mein?" Morgan asked the woman across from her.

A smile spread across Ben's lips at the sound of her voice. Concern was rampant after he'd woken up. There had been no guarantee his distraction succeeded in giving his partner the time she'd needed to escape from Sullivan's plot. But there she was, still throwing her attitude at everyone in the room like she owned the place.

"Me? I… That is…" the woman sputtered at first, pulling the container closer to her side. "I asked if anyone wanted some. Well, okay, I thought it loudly at least."

"Pass it here," Morgan said.

The woman looked familiar to Ben, but he failed to recall where they might have met before. The man at her side, though, required no introduction.

"I've got it." Kanigher wrested the container free from the woman's grasp, then handed it over.

"Thanks."

"Save some for me," Ben called from the top of the stairs.

All eyes turned to him. Forks dropped, clanging against the table. Morgan dropped noodles on the floor.

"Ben?" She jumped to her feet. Her chair crashed into the computer banks behind her. Morgan hurried up the steps. "Ben!"

She squeezed him tight. If he hadn't been injured before, he was well on his way, thanks to Morgan's exuberance.

"Hey, Morgan," he said with a smile. "Did you miss me?"

She let him go. In ten seconds flat, Morgan went from relieved partner to concerned physician. She looked him over. Her hands brushed across his side where the bullet had connected and over his cheek where the specks of brick had been embedded in his skin.

"How are you standing?" she asked, awestruck at his presence. "Your wounds? Ben, what happened?"

He caught her hand in his. Gently, he grazed her cheek and the bruise that ran near her lips. "I was going to ask the same thing."

A throat cleared behind them. Metcalf had waited long enough. Ben tried to hold back the grimace, but realized the timing of her entry was intentional to keep their conversation to a minimum. He worried that, even after everything, the stubborn woman had truly learned nothing. He worried what it meant for them going forward, if she couldn't find it in her heart to trust them.

Metcalf patted his back, then started down the steps to join the others. She grabbed an egg roll and took a bite. Ben's gaze remained locked on her, so much so that Morgan was forced to turn his attention back with a push.

"What is it?"

He shook his head and forced a grin. "We can talk about it later."

"You sure?"

There would be time for his worries another day. He had survived against all odds. It was time to enjoy the moment. That was all any of them could do now.

"Yeah," Ben said. "It's nothing."

Ben started down the steps, but Morgan hesitated. Her words caught in his ears, though he made no move to respond. "Right," she whispered. "Okay."

Slowly, she joined him at the table. Ben reached for a plate, stopped by the hand of the woman he had failed to recognize.

"Glad you made it, Agent Riley," she said. "I told you we needed you more than you needed us."

It was the woman from the mall, the one with the stroller and no baby. She had run interference against the surveillance teams following his every move. Ben had never seen her again, yet here she stood. Her hair was different. Obviously, she had worn a wig at their previous meeting, and she appeared ten years younger with her glasses on: too young to play this game.

"You?"

"Alison Adler." She took his hand and gave a firm shake. "We never had the chance to exchange names last time."

"No. We didn't."

She smiled and returned to her meal. Another hand replaced hers, this time from Kanigher.

"Good to see you, Riley."

The hand stayed between them. Ben was hesitant to respond. Kanigher had been one of the many surveilling him after his recruitment. He had worked with Stallworth, who had allied with Sullivan. They were not the best recommendations to include when trading sides. A thin glare shot toward Morgan, who couldn't help but roll her eyes.

"Shake the man's hand, Ben," she said. "He saved my life."

Ben paused for a breath, then he took the waiting hand. "Just when I thought this day couldn't get stranger."

Kanigher chuckled. "Yeah, well. Welcome to the DSA, right?"

"Is that what we are still?" Ben asked. Both men moved toward the table and the woman standing at the head.

Metcalf cold blue stare caught each of them in turn. "More than ever."

It worried him, seeing her take charge so easily after what had happened. Everything felt different now, yet she continued on as if nothing had changed. For as much as Metcalf concerned him, his excitement grew at the possibilities ahead.

"Grab a chair," Metcalf said. The screens came to life at the press of a single button, and the DSA logo beamed over them. "It's time to get back to work."

# ABOUT THE AUTHOR

Lou Paduano is the author of the Greystone series of urban fantasy adventures, which follow Detective Greg Loren and Soriya Greystone as they hunt myths, monsters, and legends in the city of Portents.

He is also the author of the conspiracy thriller series, The DSA, a serialized tale about a clandestine government agency trying to discover the true power behind humanity's future.

Lou lives with his wife and three daughters in Grand Island, NY. You can learn more about his books, including upcoming releases and free content by visiting his website at loupaduano.com.

# THE GREYSTONE SAGA

## AVAILABLE NOW

Follow the adventures of Soriya Greystone and Detective Greg Loren as they hunt dangerous myths and legends in the city of Portents.

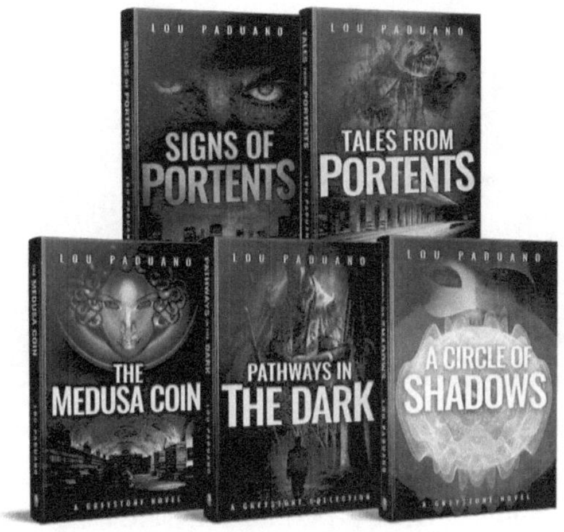


**BOOK ONE - SIGNS OF PORTENTS**
**BOOK TWO - TALES FROM PORTENTS**
**BOOK THREE - THE MEDUSA COIN**
**BOOK FOUR - PATHWAYS IN THE DARK**
**BOOK FIVE - A CIRCLE OF SHADOWS**

# GREYSTONE-IN-TRAINING

## AVAILABLE NOW

For years, Soriya trained to become the Greystone.
Follow the trials that made her the protector
Portents needed to fend off the darkest of threats.

**BOOK ONE - HAMMER AND ANVIL**
**BOOK TWO - THE GIFTS OF KALI**
**BOOK THREE - THE FINAL GAUNTLET**

# THE DSA CONTINUES IN…

*The past returns to haunt the DSA.*

On the hunt for the mysterious organization known as the Trust, Ben Riley and Morgan Dunleavy are pulled into a murder investigation. The source of their lead: Wesley Fuller, one of the first DSA agents, and a man with a hidden and troubled past.

Through him, Ben and Morgan discover more than they thought possible, including a link to a case dating back fifty years, and the secret behind a threat that has plagued the DSA for months.

Revelations come to light in this illuminating chapter of the DSA — one that points to the origins of their team as well as toward a dark and terrible future quickly heading their way.

www.ingramcontent.com/pod-product-compliance
Lightning Source LLC
Chambersburg PA
CBHW030828200726

48285CB00007B/2396